When the Wind Blows

A STIRRING TALE OF COURAGE

Anne de Waal

ISBN 9781701609747
Copyright © 2020 Anne de Waal
All rights reserved
WindSong Arts
Derby, U.K.
www.annedewaal.co.uk

NOTE FROM THE AUTHOR

Born and raised in South Africa during the Apartheid regime, I have always been utterly horrified by inequality and racism based on skin colour, religion and wealth. As a young child, I observed the mistreatment of innocent people, and these experiences haunt me to this day. I was inspired to write this novel after a visit to The National Holocaust Centre and Museum, in Laxton, England.

To my husband, Dana, my daughter Xephni and my son Duan, thank you for your help and encouragement. You remain my greatest loves, alongside Liam and Tori.

To our precious girls, Ava and Hailey, I hope you enjoy this novel. More importantly, I hope you learn from it.

You can make a difference!

This book is in memory of a baby girl with a number tattoed on her arm.

Preface

Kindertransport, meaning child transport, was a system put into place to bring more than 10 000 children to the UK. This took place in the nine months before the outbreak of World War II and included children from Germany, Austria, Czechoslovakia, and Poland. Children were placed in British foster homes.

In September 1939, just after Germany had invaded Poland, authorities imposed the wearing of a star by Jewish communities in many Polish towns. By November of the same year, all Jews over the age of ten were required to wear a 'Jewish Star'. This was a white armband, embroidered with a six-sided blue star. It was worn on the right arm over the outer garments. There were severe punishments for anyone caught not wearing it. This star and armband features in this novel.

By September 1941, all Jews over the age of six were required to wear a badge, which consisted of a yellow Star of David. This star does not feature in this tale.

Please note: For the purposes of this novel, the imposed wearing of the blue star and the time of the last Kindertransport train, does not follow the exact historical timeline.

This novel is a work of fiction. Whilst inspired by locations in Derbyshire, all names, characters, places and incidents portrayed in this book are a product of the imagination of the author.

Glossary
Tata……………….. Dad
Babcia…………….Grandmother
Dziadek…………….Grandfather

Contents

THE JOURNEYS BEGIN 1
AWAKENINGS 9
EASTWOOD HOUSE 16
BEASTS OF THE SKY 24
THREE THINGS TO REMEMBER 31
A SURPRISING DISCOVERY 37
THE END OF THE FIRST SUMMER 42
ISAAC JOINS IN. 46
WHERE IS ZIMEON? 50
A NEW CELEBRATION. 58
WHEN THE STARS WENT ON 64
A TELEGRAM ARRIVES 70
BEING THE LIGHT. 77
IN THE ICEHOUSE. 84
ISAAC IS THE LIGHT 93

Deep in the shadows of the dark,
there comes to life a tiny spark.
Though small as small the spark may be,
it lights the way for all to see.

Bill Randle.

Chapter One

THE JOURNEYS BEGIN

Isaac sat obediently and silently on the rigid, cold seat. His dark eyes were large and set deep in his thin, white face. They darted around the train carriage, watching as strangers barked out instructions. Children of all ages were being ushered into the seats around him. Some, excited and smiling, were chattering to each other. Others, like Isaac, looked fearful, lost and confused. All the children wore a nametag, and some carried small suitcases. But Isaac had no suitcase. Instead, in his hand, he clutched a small bag made of frayed fabric, which Tata had given to him that morning. Isaac knew there was a small chunk of black bread in the bag. Tata had not eaten it for breakfast, but had saved it for him to take on the journey. Although hunger gnawed at his stomach, Isaac refused to eat the bread just yet.

"Save it for later," Tata had said with a smile. "You may need it on the journey."

Seeing Isaac's nose wrinkle doubtfully, Tata had spoken again.

"Don't look so worried. You are going to have a wonderful adventure!"

Isaac had attempted a small smile to please Tata. He knew that his father was trying to be encouraging about the journey.

Through the window of the train, Isaac could see that Tata looked thin and tired. His nose was red, and his lips were grey with cold. He stamped his feet to try and keep them warm in his old, broken shoes. They were tied, not with laces, but with

THE JOURNEYS BEGIN

a piece of grimy string Isaac had found under a fence.

Tata's coat was worn, faded and threadbare. This was in stark contrast to the garishly bright blue star, newly embroidered onto a white band on his right arm. (The authorities had ordered Tata to wear the blue star.) Tata's face was lined with worry, but he was trying to look cheerful for Isaac's sake. Although he was tall, he looked vulnerable as a crowd gathered by the train and jostled him about. He blew on his pale hands to warm them, keeping his eyes on Isaac. The train hissed and puffed out a thick cloud of steam. For a second, Tata disappeared from view, but he re-appeared as the steam dissipated into the frosty air.

Isaac saw Tata nod and give a tight smile of encouragement and at that moment, it seemed to Isaac as though time slowed down. The desperate sobbing of the child sitting opposite faded away and became nothing but a distant, muffled murmur. The large lady in a green coat, who was giving booming instructions to the children, could no longer be heard as Isaac focused on keeping his eyes on Tata. Isaac had no idea when he would see his father again. He never wanted to forget his face, haggard though it was.

A piercing whistle brought the sounds and colours of the carriage rushing back to Isaac as the train jerked roughly. With a high-pitched otherworldly squeal, the wheels of the train began to turn reluctantly. Isaac's heart pounded and hurt in his chest. His breathing quickened. He sat up straight and stretched his thin neck, desperate not to lose sight of Tata.

The crowd on the platform also began to move. They pushed, shuffled and bumped each other. Tata almost disappeared as the people around him elbowed him and lifted their hands to wave and call out to their children.

The train ceased it's shuddering and began to slide along

slowly. Tata was entirely hidden in the crowd. As the train gathered speed and moved further along the track, the horde of people fell behind and stopped following. Some were crying and holding each other close for comfort. Some stood still, pale and tight-lipped whilst others waved and tried to put on a brave face and smile. Just then, the uniformed station police emerged from the official station offices shouting crudely and angrily. They began to manhandle the parents and grandparents of the children away from the platform.

Isaac searched for his father. Where was Tata? All at once, Isaac could see him. Tata had broken free of the crowd and was running along the platform beside the carriage. For a second, Isaac caught a glimpse of how Tata had been a few years ago. Tata had always loved to run. He had run freely in the countryside, his head lifted upwards as the wind blew his hair, his face glowing with good health and happiness. He would race across the hills, through dappled, shady forests, and he had won shining medals in running competitions.

But that was before the Great Sadness. Now, as Tata ran beside the train, his dark eyes, so much like Isaac's, were filled with misery. Isaac placed his hand flat on the unforgiving, cold glass of the window, reaching out to his father. Instinctively, he understood that he was not embarking upon a happy day-trip on the train. This was not going to be the cheerful adventure many of the children were expecting.

On the train rumbled, gathering speed, and on Tata ran until he reached the end of the long platform and could run no further. He stopped and bent double, struggling to catch his breath. Then panting heavily, he straightened up and lifted his arm with the white band and blue star. He waved his thin hand in farewell. Behind Tata, Isaac could see the armed station police running up the platform, blowing whistles and shouting at Tata. The train, now travelling at quite some speed, curved around a bend and in an enormous hiss of voluminous steam, Isaac lost his Tata.

*

On the highest part of the hill overlooking the village, the wind blew a chilly breeze up and over the rocks. It caught the autumn leaves and sent them dancing across the sunny path. Anna Elizabeth Eastwood called out to Shell.

"Come on, boy," she cried. "It's time to go home. Mrs Turner will not be happy if we keep her waiting."

Mrs Turner was the house-keeper at Eastwood House, where Anna Elizabeth lived with her Father and Mother and her brother Joseph. The large, imposing, family home lay nestled on the other side of the hill.

Shell, the silky, black Cocker Spaniel came dashing over the hill towards Anna Elizabeth. She had been standing on what she called 'the lookout rock'. Stepping down from the large slab of jutting flat rock, from which she believed she could see the whole world, she bent down and rubbed him vigorously. He wagged his tail and tried to reach up to lick her face. Anna Elizabeth fastened his lead to his collar then stood up to take one last look at the village in the valley. The church steeple stood tall and beautiful in the bright autumn morning, and she could just make out the figure of old Mr Trot making his way up the stone path as he went to unlock the church door. The ladies from the village would be meeting there at midday, as they did every week, to discuss events such as music concerts and games evenings held in the village. They took their job very seriously!

Then she noticed the Good Doctor walking past the pub and she watched as he turned in at the cottage belonging to Mr and Mrs Jenkins. Tall, with dark hair and dark eyes, gold-rimmed round spectacles and a briefcase, he took long strides up to the front door. She watched as he knocked on the door. As it opened, he disappeared inside. Anna Elizabeth wondered if one of the children might be ill. Mr and Mrs Jenkins had three children, each of whom had magnificent red hair. Anna Elizabeth always felt envious of their auburn locks. Father loved her long, brown hair, but Anna Elizabeth thought it would be so much nicer to have a head of vibrant, fiery, red curls! The Jenkins children were all like tiny, spirited, glowing volcanoes, and Anna Elizabeth loved them! She hoped all was well in the Jenkins household.

Remembering that Mrs Turner would soon have elevenses ready in the front room, she turned and ran down the sloping hill to where she joined a tree-lined path that led to the large house. As she reached the gravel drive, she was surprised to see her older brother Joseph coming around the side of the house.

"Oh hello!" said Anna Elizabeth. "Where have you been?"

"Oh," said Joseph waving his hand dismissively, "just helping out here and there…"

Anna Elizabeth was surprised. She had never known Joseph

to be willing to help out anywhere on the estate before, nor had she seen him with such shining eyes! It puzzled her, but she said nothing. She followed Joseph into the bright hall where she took off her stout boots and put them in the cupboard to be polished. She hung her coat on a hook and put her hat and scarf on the hallstand. Shell barked. He had been waiting patiently, and at last, she took off his lead and he dashed off into the kitchen. Anna Elizabeth ran upstairs to go and wash her face and hands. She frowned when she saw how wild her hair looked. She was going to struggle to get a brush through those windblown locks, but Mother was very strict about cleanliness and tidiness at elevenses.

Just after eleven, Anna Elizabeth, with her hair tidied and her face rosy from the run across the hills, walked into the front room. To her surprise and joy, she saw that Father was there. (Father was often away from home. He spent a lot of his time working in London.) Anna Elizabeth was about to run towards him when she saw how serious his face looked. She stopped and stood still, looking to Mother for reassurance, but Mother's face was serious too. Anna Elizabeth was even more confused when she saw that all the staff except for Lisi were gathered in the room. Thay had never joined the family for elevenses before. Mother put her finger to her lips to show Anna Elizabeth to keep silent. The radio was on, and everyone seemed to be listening intently.

Shell ran in at that moment. He was oblivious to the solemn atmosphere and eager to be petted, but no one except Anna Elizabeth noticed him. Momentarily distracted, she knelt to stroke the spaniel, but she lifted her head and was riveted to the sound on the radio when she heard a voice say:

"…consequently, this country is at war with Germany."

Mother caught in her breath and put her handkerchief over

her mouth. Mrs Turner's head hung as she shook it slowly from side to side. Joseph came into the room and looked surprised to see everyone looking so serious.

'What's the matter?" he asked, concerned.

No-one answered him. The parlour, usually a room filled with laughter and conversation, was silent. Finally, Father lifted his head and looked across at his son.

"We're at war, Joseph. The worst has happened."

Walking over to Mother, Father bent to kiss her head. She looked up, her pale eyes clouded with worry.

"I must get to London immediately, Grace. There is no time to lose."

He straightened up, standing tall and proud. Then he turned abruptly and left the room. Anna Elizabeth saw him disappear into his study. He locked the door behind him. For as long as Anna Elizabeth could remember, Father rarely closed the door, but today it was shut fast. Elevenses seemed to have been forgotten, and Anna Elizabeth found herself alone, as the adults left one by one. She stood silently. A murky darkness seemed to settle over the room, even though the sun still shone brightly. Shell whined.

Later that evening, Anna Elizabeth stood with Shell by her bedroom window upstairs and looked down to the gravel drive, where she could see Father speaking to Mother. Often at this time of the evening, Anna Elizabeth and Father took a walk across the hills with Shell. She knew the first lights would be coming on in some of the houses in the village and thin spires of smoke would be wafting into the evening air. The reflection of the setting sun would have turned the silver lake into a fiery red, and hundreds of birds would be settling into the pine trees for the night.

But this evening, they would not be walking together hand

in hand, laughing and talking, with Shell sniffing around their feet. She watched as Father turned and looked up and waved to her. She blew him a kiss and waved back. Then he turned away from her, and putting on his hat, bent down to slide into the shining black car that had arrived to collect him.

Anna Elizabeth thought that her Mother looked unusually small and vulnerable, so she was pleased when she saw her brother Joseph emerge from the house and stand beside Mother. He put a protective arm around her shoulders. The man driving the car said something to Mother, and she nodded. The car pulled away and drove smoothly down the drive. Anna Elizabeth could just see it as it curved through the misty avenue of trees. And then it was gone.

*

Isaac had not eaten for hours. His head hurt, and he felt sick. The boat rolled from side to side. Isaac thought this terrible journey would never end. First, the train, and now, a boat. He rubbed his eyes, and for a second, a vision of Mama flashed before him. In that moment, he longed for her to place her cool, healing hand on his fevered forehead, but then she was gone again. He heard a terrible wailing sound, but it was a moment before he realised that it came from his own throat. It scared him, and he began to shake. He did not want to make that awful noise again. The large lady in the green coat came hurrying over.

"Hush, hush," she whispered, not unkindly. "Soon we will be there and you will begin to feel better."

As he looked at her through hazy eyes, he wondered what it meant to feel better. He wanted Tata. He wanted Mama. The pain in his head grew worse, but Isaac said not a word.

Chapter Two

AWAKENINGS

The sun was coming over the brows of the hills in the distance, and a flock of geese rose, flapping their wings noisily above the misty, silver lake. In a stone cottage at the edge of the village, three children with flaming, red hair stared wide-eyed into the wooden cot in which all new babies in the family had slept.

"All is well!" said the Good Doctor drying his hands on a clean towel. It's been a long night, but all is well."

"Thank you, Doctor," said Mr Jenkins. "I am so grateful you were on hand to help."

Mrs Jenkins sipped a cup of tea and smiled down at the cot.

"I wonder what names we should choose?" she said.

Matthew, the eldest Jenkins boy, put his hand into the cot and stroked a tiny, soft, silky head.

"This one should be called Tiger. He looks just like a tiger."

"Good idea!" giggled Maisy softly.

She pointed at a black kitten next to the striped Tiger.

"We could call this one Mr Wriggle, because he never stops wriggling!"

Everyone giggled. Time had slowed down in the Jenkins household while the kittens were born. The family did not yet know of the shadow looming over England, which had grown very dark in the last few hours.

"Well," said the Good Doctor, "I am going to leave you all to take care of the new feline family members and make my way home. I am sure Mrs Bray has already got my breakfast porridge ready."

The Good Doctor had moved into the village a short while ago, and he lived in a stone house, which belonged to old Mrs Bray. Mr Bray had died several years ago. The Good Doctor helped Mrs Bray around the house and garden, and she took great delight in taking care of him. He helped pay the rent, and his small room at the back of the house had a little study attached to it. He often worked there until late in the night.

"Thanks again," said Mr Jenkins. "When poor Mittens got into trouble delivering her kittens, and I couldn't find the vet, I was worried."

"I am glad I could help," said the Good Doctor smiling.

His blue eyes crinkled kindly as he smiled, ruffling the hair of the youngest Jenkins boy, Max, in the arms of Mr Jenkins.

"Look after those little kittens, now will you?" said the Good Doctor kindly.

Everyone nodded and smiled and called out their thanks and goodbyes as he pulled the door closed behind him, and made his way into the main street of the village.

He walked past the church where Mr Trot was raking up the fallen autumn leaves.

"Mornin' Doc," he called out. "You're up early!"

"Indeed," smiled the Good Doctor. "Mittens got into a spot of trouble yesterday with her kittens, and the vet is away in Bexton for the week."

"Eee!" said Mr Trot. "Is she better now?"

"Oh, yes," said the Good Doctor. "Five beautiful kittens she has. One for each member of the family."

Mr Trot laughed, his broad smile showing his missing teeth. He waved as the Good Doctor went on his way.

Down past the village green, he walked with a jaunty stride, until he neared the village school, which was tightly closed. It would soon be filled with chattering infants and juniors, but for now, it was silent. He walked beyond the Crinkle Crankle wall by the big house. Evergreen ivy tumbled down the side of the wall. To his left a small hill rose upwards and coming over the top of it, he saw Anna Elizabeth appear with Shell, her beautiful, friendly, black spaniel. As the Good Doctor walked on, she ran down the hill with Shell, past the old disused icehouse. They met at the gate where the stone wall at the edge of the field joined the road.

"Isn't it a beautiful morning?" called the Good Doctor.

Anna Elizabeth drew up beside him. He put his hand over the wall to stroke Shell, who was trying to stretch over the drystone walling.

"I..., I'm not sure," said Anna Elizabeth hesitantly.

"Whatever do you mean?" asked the Good Doctor.

"Well... you know... the war!"

The Good Doctor looked sharply at Anna Elizabeth.

"What are you saying," he asked, his head tilted enquiringly.

"We're at war now," said Anna Elizabeth. "I heard it yesterday on the radio, and now Father has gone away, and Mother cries a lot, and Joseph is all secretive, and no-one will tell me anything."

Anna Elizabeth looked at the Good Doctor. The colour had drained from his face. Shell barked, puzzled that the Good Doctor was not giving him any more attention.

"I did not know," the Good Doctor said. "I have been busy since early yesterday morning! I did not know."

The Good Doctor was shocked. Anna Elizabeth had never seen him like this before.

"This is terrible," he said. "So terrible!"

Shaking his head, he set off, lurching awkwardly, as though his legs were not steady.

AWAKENINGS

Anna Elizabeth watched him, mystified, before walking towards the wooden gate. Today, she thought, she would make her way home from her early morning walk, through the village.

*

Isaac felt listless. They had been on a train, and a boat, and now they were about to get onto another train! He heard his name called out. He had been sitting still for so long he found it hard to move. The tall girl next to him nudged him.

"That's you," she hissed.

He stood up, easing his stiffened joints and started to move forward. A lady wearing red lipstick smiled at him. He stared at her lips. Mama had once worn red lipstick. She had been so happy that night. Her dark hair had shone, and her black eyes had glinted. She had worn a pink, sparkling dress that floated like a misty cloud as she walked, and her silk stockings had made a dark line on the back of her calves. Tata had glowed that night too. He had held Mama in his arms, and they had whirled around the small living room together. They had picked up Isaac and danced with him too. Their laughter had rung through the room, and Mama had planted a kiss on Isaac's cheek. The red lipstick had left the mark of the kiss on his face.

"Don't rub it off," she had giggled. "That will remind you of my love all evening!"

She and Tata had stepped out into the street, and Isaac had watched as they walked jauntily down to the bus stop. He would be staying with Babcia, his grandmother, but he did not mind so much. He had Mama's kiss on his face. But that was before the Great Sadness. The memory faded, and he blinked.

"Come along," said the red lips before him now.

His body was aching, and he did not want to go, but he clutched his bag and followed the lady. All around him, people were speaking, but he could not understand what they were saying. The red lips led him, and a number of other children, across a busy road and into yet another station. It was a bustling! People in dark coats were rushing all around him. Everything seemed grey. He shivered, but his eyes were drawn to the lady with the red lips, who seemed to stand out in the colourless crowd. Those smiling, red lips seemed like his Mama beckoning, calling, so he followed. She led him and the other children onto a big, steaming train.

As the children stepped wearily up into the carriage, she spoke.

"This is the last bit of the journey," she said. "We are almost there."

But Isaac and many of the children did not speak English.

"If only I could understand what she was saying," thought Isaac helplessly.

He settled himself into a seat, and the train pulled out of the dark, sooty station.

Beside him, a tall, thin girl struggled to hold a screaming infant. Isaac stared at the girl who was trying to calm the small child by jiggling it up and down on her knee. The girl seemed close to tears herself. Isaac turned and curled up against the window, trying to shut out the angry screams. He ignored the hunger gripping his stomach. As the train rumbled on and on, past dull grey houses streaked with soot, Isaac found himself drifting off into a dreamless sleep.

He had no idea how long he had slept, but on waking, he found the picture through the window had changed. They were in the countryside and a patchwork of green and yellow hills flashed by, stretched out like the quilt Babcia had made him years ago. Trees and hedges accentuated the edges of the squares of the patchwork countryside. Here and there a house, or a church steeple peeping through golden trees caught his eye.

"Here you go, luv. Have a biscuit."

The lady with the red lips was cheerfully holding out a tin filled with pale yellow biscuits. Isaac took one and began to nibble on the corner. Then, a man gave him a tin cup with water in it. Isaac gulped it down and began to feel slightly better.

*

Anna Elizabeth followed Lisi, the maid, into the large spare room on the third floor. She carried three pillows, and Lisi had an armful of extra blankets. Lisi dumped them onto one of the beds and walked over to the windows. She reached up and pulled a deep red, silk cord, and long, thick curtains dragged heavily across to reveal tall, glass windows overlooking the side terrace of the house. Peering out, Anna Elizabeth could see Mary, the cook, picking the last of the summer herbs in the kitchen garden, for their dinner. She turned away from the window.

"How many children are coming?" she asked Lisi.

"I'm not sure," replied Lisi as she pushed a stray piece of hair from her eyes and tucked it into the knot at the back of her head. She bent to start making up the beds.

"Mrs Turner only said to make up all the spare beds."

"I wonder how old they are and if they will be boys or girls."

Anna Elizabeth felt excited at the thought of so many children coming to stay. What fun! But Lisi cast a shadow on her joy.

"You will have to be very kind. These children will be sad. They have suffered things of which we know nothing!"

Anna Elizabeth stopped short and stared in surprise. In that subdued moment, Shell burst into the room and ran to Anna Elizabeth wagging his tail. As she bent to stroke him, she wondered what terrible things the children might have seen.

"Why have the children suffered?" she asked, looking up at Lisi.

"I don't want to say now," replied Lisi, and a small frown pulled her eyebrows together briefly. "Come now. You can help me."

She smiled kindly at Anna Elizabeth.

"We must make this a good place for the children."

The sun came out from behind the clouds, and a shaft of sunlight lit the room.

"Ugh!" said Anna Elizabeth. "That sunbeam shows up every speck of dust. I'll get a duster and clean it."

She and Shell scurried down the stairs together.

"Come on, Shell. Let's make the spare rooms shine."

CHAPTER THREE

EASTWOOD HOUSE

Isaac's eyes were open wide with interest! He had never been in a car before! The smooth, red seats felt cold against his thin legs. He could not see out of the silver-lined windows as he was in the middle of the back seat, between the other children who were older and taller than he was. On one side of him sat the tall girl with the grisly infant. He felt sorry for her. She looked exhausted. Her hair hung like tiny rats' tails from beneath her felt hat. Her eyes had red rings, and her white face was thin and pointed.

The infant had started moaning again, and Isaac wished he had a handkerchief to clean its wet face and streaming nose. He was sure that it would bring comfort to the baby. Tata always used to have a handkerchief for noses and faces! It did not matter where they went or where they were, Tata always had a handkerchief in his pocket, for tears. Its soft, white linen never failed to dry sniffles, ease sadness and make Isaac smile.

Exhausted, the tall girl did nothing to try and comfort the child. Her arms lay limply around the baby, and she no longer made any attempt to pacify her.

On the other side of Isaac sat a girl who clutched a small pink bag on her lap. She began to talk to the tall girl on the other side of Isaac.

"I hope there will be someone to help with the baby when we get there," she said. "What is her name?"

"Her name is Marta," said the tall girl.

Then, she pointed to herself.

"I'm Gisela and those two in front are my brothers, Zimeon and Jacov. They are twins."

Isaac felt a small glimmer of interest when he heard the boys in front were twins, but the girl next to him went on talking.

"I'm Kornelia," she said. "You are lucky to be all together. I am all alone."

She cast her eyes down sadly and rather dramatically, before turning to look at Isaac.

"Who are you?" she asked.

Isaac tried to tell her, but to his surprise, no sound came from his throat. He tried again, but he felt as though words would choke him. He blinked three times to clear the mist from his eyes, and then picking up the card around his neck, on which his name was written, he showed Kornelia. She glanced at him sharply and then read the words on his card out loud.

"Isaac Baranek," she announced to everyone.

She turned back to him and spoke in a bold voice.

"How old are you?"

Isaac opened his mouth, but again he choked. He put his hand to his mouth and stared at her with frightened eyes. She snatched up his name card impatiently.

"Oh!" she said, reading it. "You are ten. What a baby. I'm almost twelve."

Whenever Isaac had met people before, they would all smile at each other, but today was different. It felt to Isaac as though the Great Sadness was new all over again. No one could smile. Isaac shrank down in his seat, feeling miserable.

He did not see Kornelia roll her eyes at Gisela over his head, and he did not see Gisela turn her head away from Kornelia to look out of the window. Suddenly the twins called out.

"See there... it's a big house!"

Isaac sat up straight and stretched his thin neck to try and see out of the windows. But he was so small that he could not see much.

The car rolled smoothly up to the tall house and stopped gently. The engine fell silent. The man, who had been driving, climbed out. He went around to open the door on Gisela's side. He helped her as she struggled out with the baby in her arms. Isaac slid along the seat and got out beside Kornelia. His feet crunched on the gravel. Despite the sunshine, the frosty ice between the tiny stones made his feet feel cold through his worn shoes. The house cast a large, dark shadow over the drive where they stood. He shivered as the icy air touched his skinny throat. He tried to pull his skimpy scarf more tightly around his neck.

All at once, a loud scream rang out, and Isaac jumped with fright. The large, front door of the big house had opened, and a black dog had come bounding down the stairs towards the six children with their bundles, bags and suitcases.

"Oh, oh, take him away, take him away, aaaarghh!" screamed Kornelia.

She tried to get back inside the car to hide from the dog. For the first time in many hours, Isaac felt a muscle pull at the corner of his mouth. He almost grinned, but he stopped himself.

"What a baby she is," he thought as he turned from staring at the terrified Kornelia. He bent to stroke the excited, black spaniel.

Shell's dark eyes were gentle. He had a white, shell-shaped mark on his chest. The spaniel wagged his tail and licked Isaac's hand in welcome.

Isaac heard the voices all around him, but he kept his face down, close to the warm, silky head of the spaniel. He was

When the Stars Went On

unwilling to face the rest of the world just yet, and the cacophony of chatter bothered him. Then, he heard a clear voice.

"Hello. I'm Anna Elizabeth."

Still crouching beside Shell, he lifted his eyes and looked up. There, framed in the pale, lemon light of the autumn sun, stood a girl. He guessed she must have been about his age. She had long, brown hair tied back with a large, red satin bow. Her eyes were a sparkling, pale blue and lined with dark lashes. Her chin tilted slightly and made her dimpled smile more radiant. Her bright, red, knitted jumper reflected the red of her lips and the healthy rosiness of her cheeks. A white, lace collar framed her face.

"What is your name?" she asked, smiling.

Isaac did not understand what she was saying. But even if he had, it would not have mattered, as he found himself unable to speak to reply.

"He no talk," he heard Kornelia say in broken English. "He no talk for days."

Isaac felt like growling with rage at Kornelia. He wanted to say something to the beautiful Anna Elizabeth, but before he could try, he was interrupted by the loud wails of baby Marta. Lisi, coming down the stone stairs, moved swiftly towards the exhausted Gisela and took the screaming Marta from her. She spoke to the children in Polish.

"Come," she said kindly. "Follow me."

Anna Elizabeth stared in surprise. She had known Lisi had been born in another country, but she had not thought about the fact that she could speak another language so fluently.

The children looked relieved to hear someone speaking Polish. Holding their possessions close, they started to move towards the house. The twins walked beside Anna Elizabeth's older brother Joseph, who had come out to welcome the children. Kornelia had attached herself to Mrs Turner, the housekeeper, and she clung to her plump arm, keeping a wary eye out for the wagging tail and the pink tongue of the excited spaniel, Shell.

"Come on!" said Anna Elizabeth to Isaac. "I'll show you to your room."

She whistled to Shell and, he followed her, wagging his tail. Walking beside them, Isaac felt the knot in his stomach begin to ease. They mounted the stairs to the front door, which was standing wide open. They stepped into the hall. Isaac's eyes flicked around the room, examining and probing every corner of the warm space that appeared before him.

To his left, three large oak doors stood open. One room was dark, but the other two were brightly lit and, Isaac could see a long table, already laid for dinner. He wondered who could be grand enough to eat at such an impressive table under such a glittering chandelier. In the next room, Isaac could see a large, green velvet chair as well as a vast piano and bronze music stand. For a second, his throat contracted. Mama had played the flute and Dziadek, his grandfather, always accompanied her on the piano in their small flat. Isaac had loved spending long evenings listening to the music while Babcia, his Grandmother, darned socks or mended trousers. In his mind's eye, he could see Tata sitting in his favourite chair, relaxed and happy, his long limbs stretched out in front of him, as the music flowed gently over them, like the soft, warm waves he had known by the lake in summer. But that was before the Great Sadness. Isaac turned his head sharply. He did not want to remember.

His eyes darted to his right where yet another oak door marked the entrance to another room.

"That is Father's study," said Anna Elizabeth. "Father is not here right now."

Isaac stared at her, not understanding. Further into the hall, a warm fire crackled and popped in a huge fireplace. Isaac felt that it relieved the grandeur of the space in which he found himself. It made the enormous room feel cosy. That, and the thick, patterned, red carpet. And Shell, of course. Shell nudged his wet nose into Isaac's hand. Isaac stroked his head and found comfort in the warm silkiness of the little curls around Shell's ears.

"We are going upstairs," Anna Elizabeth said.

She pointed towards the large, wooden staircase at the end of the room. Shell dashed ahead, and Isaac felt less nervous about moving up into the house with Shell peering down at him and encouraging his every step upwards with gentle, excited barks. Up and up they went until they reached the third floor. They walked along a quiet, carpeted corridor and Anna Elizabeth led Isaac to the last door, which opened into a large bedroom. The twins were already there. They were each sitting cross-legged on a bed.

"You can have that bed," said Zimeon in Polish pointing to the bed by the window. "Jacov and I would like to be together here."

Isaac walked over to the bed by the window and stood staring at it, not knowing what to do next. Anna Elizabeth opened the top-drawer of a large, oak chest of drawers.

"You can put your bag in here," she said.

She patted inside the drawer and pointed to his bag to show him what she meant.

Isaac understood, and for the first time since leaving Poland, he let go of the bag Tata had given him. Then, to explain where he should hang his outdoor clothing, Anna Elizabeth, mimed taking off his scarf and jacket and she showed him where to hang them. He slowly unwound his scarf and took off his jacket. Like his father's coat, Isaac's sleeve had a white armband and blue embroidered star. He stood on his toes and stretched to reach the hook on the bedroom door to hang up his coat and scarf. The twins did the same with their jackets although they did not have the embroidered star on their jacket sleeves.

Deep in the house, a gong sounded.

"That will be the supper gong," said Anna Elizabeth leading the way. "I bet you are all ravenous!"

*

Much later that evening, Isaac lay in the semi-darkness of his new bedroom. He was warmer and more comfortable than he had been in many months. The lamp on the table beside his bed gifted a cosy, golden light to the room. He was still amazed that he had been invited into the grand dining room. He had been seated on a chair beside Anna Elizabeth, and Shell had stayed by his feet. Every time Isaac had put his hand down, Shell had given him a gentle lick as if to say, "You can relax. I'm here."

When the Stars Went On

But Isaac had struggled to eat. It had been so long since he had eaten a proper meal and every mouthful made him want to gag. He kept thinking of how Tata had told him to be polite and to eat whatever was placed before him, but although he had tried, he had not managed to touch his food at all.

And now his stomach ached. He looked over at the twins. They had decided to sleep in one bed and were fast asleep, their arms around each other. Isaac's tummy rumbled, and he suddenly thought of the piece of black bread Tata had saved for him. Quietly, he pushed back the covers of the bed. He swung his thin legs over the edge and tiptoed across the thick carpet to the chest of drawers. He slowly pulled open the heavy, top drawer and reached in to retrieve his small, frayed fabric bag. He carried it back to his bed. Kneeling on the white sheets, he began to untie the string that held it closed. As the fabric bag fell open, the piece of black bread rolled out into Isaac's hand, and he hungrily lifted it to his mouth. But something else caught his eye as the bag lay open. It was a something small and white. Clean and neatly folded into a square, lay Tata's handkerchief.

Isaac froze and stared at it in disbelief. Silently, he put the black bread down, his hunger forgotten. His eyes remained fixed on the handkerchief. He put his hand into the bag, and his thumb and fingers gently touched the smooth edge of the folded, white linen. He stroked it and felt how it had been washed until it was soft. He held it to his face and breathed in deeply. He could smell Tata. Suddenly the tears spilt down his cheeks. For a long, long time, Isaac lay in the golden semi-darkness, clutching the white handkerchief to his face. Sobs wracked his small, thin body. But it was no good. This time, the white handkerchief did not dry his tears or take his deep longing and sadness away.

CHAPTER FOUR

BEASTS OF THE SKY

"When can I meet the children staying at your house?" asked Maisy Jenkins.

Several weeks had passed by, and she and Anna Elizabeth were trudging across the village green towards the Jenkins' cottage after school. Anna Elizabeth shrugged her shoulders.

"Mother says we must give them time to settle in first. And, she says she wants to make sure they have some new clothes. Poor Isaac has very little with him, and Mother says she cannot let him out in this weather without warm shoes."

"Will they come to school with us?"

"Mother says the three boys will. But she says the oldest girl, Gisela, will stay at home and help Lisi to look after baby Marta. Mother says she will help Gisela with her studies. And of course, Kornelia will go to the secondary school in Wickley."

"Poor Kornelia!" said Maisy. "She will have to catch the bus with Big Andy."

Anna Elizabeth giggled.

"Yes. Poor Kornelia. I would not like to catch the bus with Big Andy. He scares me a little, especially when he walks through the village after he has played in a rugby match. He is so big and burly. When he struts along importantly, all covered in mud, and carrying his rugby ball under his arm like a little round pig, I always cross the street so that I don't have to talk to him!"

The girls shuddered and then giggled.

"Anyway, Mother says that Isaac will not be allowed to

When the Stars Went On

leave the house until he has a new coat. She says she simply will not allow him out wearing a coat with a star on the sleeve. But Isaac refuses to let her take the coat."

Maisy frowned.

"A star?" she asked. "What is wrong with a star?"

"I'm not really sure," replied Anna Elizabeth, "but I saw Lisi cry when she saw it on his jacket. Not all the children had a star, but Lisi says they were just lucky! Anyway, Kornelia's coat is new and smart, but poor Isaac's is threadbare. Mother wanted to burn it, but Isaac would not let her take it, so it is still hanging in his room."

The girls had reached the Jenkins' stone cottage, and Maisy begged Anna Elizabeth to come in to see the kittens.

"You will love them!" she coaxed.

And Anna Elizabeth did. She cooed over the tiny, mewing kittens and stroked their soft fur.

"I wish I could bring Isaac to see them," she said, holding Mr Wriggle up to cuddle.

"Oh, do!" begged Maisy. "I so want to meet him, and I'm sure he will love the kittens."

At that moment, the door opened, and Matthew walked in from school. He flung his books down and threw himself into a chair by the fire.

"You look as though you have not had a good day," said Maisy putting Tiger back into the bed beside Mittens.

Matthew grunted sulkily and ran his hand through his red hair.

"We got issued with our gas masks today."

"What do you mean?" asked Maisy.

"Stupid war!" said Matthew. "We all have to carry gas masks with us, in case there is a poison gas attack."

Maisy and Anna Elizabeth turned and stared at him with

round eyes.

"Where is your mask?" asked Anna Elizabeth softly.

"I left it in the shed," said Matthew. "It is so ugly and smelly, and I did not want Max to see it and be scared."

Maisy and Anna Elizabeth looked at each other.

"Do you think we will get gas masks too?" asked Anna Elizabeth turning back to the disgruntled Matthew.

"Of course, you will," scoffed Matthew with all the wisdom of being in secondary school and older than the girls. "Do you think the poison gas will stop before it reaches you?" he said sarcastically, and he gave a grown-up guffaw.

"What will the gas do if it reaches us?" asked Maisy nervously.

But this time, Matthew would not answer her question. He said nothing. He stared into the fire, and he stayed silent, lost deep in his own thoughts. A morbid stillness descended on the room, and Anna Elizabeth suddenly felt cold.

"I think I should go home," she said, aware that the mood in the cottage had changed.

She put on her coat, eager to leave as soon as she could. She wanted to walk back up the hill, and she wanted to find Shell. She would walk with him through the avenue of trees as she did most evenings, and he would stand with her on the lookout rock as she watched the geese flying across the silver lake. She wanted to forget that a war had started. She wanted to forget that there were sad children living in her home reminding her, in every waking moment of the day, that misery seemed to be all around her. She wanted to forget that Father was not coming home again tonight. She did not want to hear Marta crying for her Mama. She did not want to look into the lost eyes of the twins, nor did she want to listen to Kornelia, pretending she was not homesick and boasting of her old life in Poland.

When the Stars Went On

The winter sun was dropping rapidly down behind the trees when Anna Elizabeth waved good-bye to Maisy. She walked as fast as she could towards the path that would take her up the hill and home again. It did not take her long to reach Eastwood House, and she pushed open the front door and called out to Shell.

"Shell, come here boy."

He did not come running to her as he always did. She picked up his lead from the hall stand, and began to look for him. Puzzled, she walked through the rooms on the lower floor, searching for him and calling his name. He was nowhere to be found. She decided to ask Mary, the cook.

"Mary?" she called as she pushed open the door leading to the kitchen. "Mary, have you seen Shell?"

But there was no need for Mary to answer her, for on the mat by the kitchen fire, lay Shell on his back, with Isaac tickling his tummy. Shell was wholly engrossed in the attention he was receiving and did not move when Anna Elizabeth walked in.

"Shell," said Anna Elizabeth sharply. "Come here!"

At the sound of her voice, Shell immediately rolled over, but he took his time about leaving his comfortable spot by the fire. Slowly, and somewhat sheepishly, he made his way over to Anna Elizabeth, his tail wagging from side to side. Anna Elizabeth felt exceedingly irritated. She grabbed his collar and attached the lead.

"I'm taking *my* dog for a walk," she told Mary shortly, and she glared at Isaac.

She turned swiftly and walked away, ignoring the confusion in the eyes of both Mary and Isaac. She stormed out of the house. Hot tears stung her eyes, and her heart beat powerfully in her chest. She half walked, half ran through the avenue of leafless trees. Usually, in the winter, she delighted in staring up at the boughs of black, lacy twigs, silhouetted against the wintery sky. But this evening, all she could see materialising in ghostly form before her eyes, were the faces of six skinny, unhappy children wearing gas masks! Shell ran along beside her, his silky ears flapping, his sleek fur rippling.

Anna Elizabeth turned and Shell turned with her. He knew the path as well as she did. They sped on up the hill so that Anna Elizabeth could reach her favourite lookout point. From up there she could usually see the whole village, and across to the forests on the other side of the water.

But tonight, a low-lying, thick fog was creeping stealthily in from the iron-grey lake and obstructing her view of the village. She stood silently. Her breathing was fast and angry. The sun was almost completely gone, and the last rays of red and pale yellow merged with scudding, charcoal clouds and the deep purple sky. The forest by the lake looked black, menacing and cold.

She hoped the geese would soon fly over. The sound of their sociable cries and the sight of them flying in perfect formation never failed to take her breath away and lift her spirits.

But the geese were silent tonight, and nowhere to be seen. Anna Elizabeth stared grimly into the distance, waiting... waiting.

Where were the geese?

And then she heard it. A low drone. It started faintly at first and was almost indiscernible. It grew louder. And louder. Shell jumped up and barked. Anna Elizabeth was afraid. The wind whipped wildly at her hair, and the thick fog began creeping up the hill, sending thin, icy tendrils to catch at her feet. The drone became deafening as it began to echo around the valley. Anna Elizabeth trembled, feeling as though she was about to be swallowed by a mighty, roaring beast.

When the Stars Went On

Suddenly, in the distance, in the exact spot in the sky that Anna Elizabeth was searching for the geese, and flying in perfect formation, she saw it. A squadron of black-bellied planes. As they came closer, the noise increased, and the wind tore at her hair. Shell barked and barked frantically. Anna Elizabeth fell to her knees, ducked down and buried her face into his fur. The advancing planes roared overhead. The propellers droned, and the engines thundered. The sound was intolerable. The whole valley seemed to shake and rumble in shock and fear.

And then it was all over. As quickly as it had started, the drone subsided. Anna Elizabeth, still clinging to Shell, lifted her head. Seeing that the sky overhead was clear, she stood up, her legs trembling. She watched as the planes disappeared into the distance. Looking down, she spotted a few comforting village lights appearing through the fog, but her heart continued to race. Although Anna Elizabeth could not possibly know it, she had witnessed the first of many squadrons of planes that would fly over the valley.

"Come on, Shell," she said, her voice quivering. "Let's go home."

Together they raced back down the hill and up through the avenue of trees. They all but fell through the front door and into the hall. The Kindertransport children were gathered there together. It was almost time for supper. Baby Marta was toddling around, and laughing as the twins pretended to chase her. Gisela and Kornelia were pouring over a book together by the hallstand. Isaac was staring up at a large painting on the wall beside Father's office.

The calm, happy atmosphere in the room caused Anna Elizabeth to stop abruptly and gather her thoughts. She remembered how furious she had been before leaving the house on her walk. Isaac turned to her and caught her eye. She stood still for a moment, feeling her fear and anger dissipate in the warm hall. She blinked and smiled at him, apologetically. She bent down and loosened the lead on Shell's collar and allowed him to run across to Isaac. He knelt to catch Shell. As usual, Isaac said nothing and his face remained almost expressionless. But his nose wrinkled and it was as if a tiny light had begun to shine from somewhere deep inside of him.

As she watched him bending to stroke Shell, Anna Elizabeth understood that the joy Shell brought into Eastwood House was not just for her. She knew now that she would have to share him with this small, lost boy from a faraway land; this boy who could not speak because of the sadness deep inside of him. It was a sadness she did not understand. As she watched, Shell licked the end of Isaac's nose. Anna Elizabeth realised as she watched them playing, that this was the first time in weeks, that she had seen Isaac smile!

CHAPTER FIVE

THREE THINGS TO REMEMBER

Anna Elizabeth never forgot that wild night out on the hill when the planes replaced the geese in the angry sky above the lake. She also never forgot the light in Isaac's dark eyes as his face relaxed into the first smile she had seen since he had arrived. She had experienced something that, without her knowing or understanding right then, would begin to shape her life and teach her things she had not known before. She had started a journey on which she would piece together the puzzle of understanding the experiences of the six young strangers in her home. Experiences, which lay deep in their hearts, of which she knew nothing.

Isaac never forgot the sense of relief he felt when Anna Elizabeth, with her hair wild and windblown, had looked deep into his eyes from across the room. In that moment he knew Anna Elizabeth understood something about him. He could not explain it, but he knew that she had glimpsed his past. But, more importantly, Isaac also knew that she did not begrudge him a place in the heart of her beloved Shell!

After that, Isaac found that life settled into a comfortable routine. Every morning, he and Anna Elizabeth would take Shell for a brief walk down the long drive of the big house. Through Shell, Isaac discovered that he loved to run. He and Shell would break away from Anna Elizabeth as she dreamily wandered through the avenue of trees, and together they would run. Isaac's heart would pound fast as the wind pulled his hair away from his face. He felt his shoulders relax as he tilted his head back. It seemed to him that as long as he was running with Shell, out in the open air, the Great Sadness faded in his mind, and left space for him to see fragments of light and colour again.

In the mornings, after breakfast, the children would set off for school. Kornelia would take a different path to catch the bus to Wickley. The twins would walk with Anna Elizabeth and Isaac as they made their way down to the school in the village. All the children were issued with gas masks. Anna Elizabeth kept having nightmares about her ugly mask, but Mother told her it might save her life one day. So, each child obediently carried a box with a gas mask in it, everywhere they went.

Many afternoons were spent playing with the Jenkins children, or quietly sitting with Shell, by the fire in the kitchen. Isaac loved the warm, comforting smells of the food Mary made, and he loved listening to her endless chatter. She never asked him questions, so he was not obliged to try and answer her. Isaac still could not speak. Although he had many thoughts and ideas, words got caught in his throat. No one seemed to mind except for Kornelia, who would repeatedly ask him questions. When he struggled and choked to make himself understood, she would sigh impatiently and answer for him.

On Friday evenings, the Good Doctor would come to the house and together with the children and Lisi, would celebrate Shabbat in the dining room. Everyone in the household was invited, and Anna Elizabeth loved listening to the prayers recited by the Good Doctor. It was always a warm and happy time.

Evenings, during the week, were spent preparing for school the next day. Most nights before bed, Mrs Eastwood, Anna Elizabeth's mother, would gather the children around her to read to them. Isaac still did not understand the words of the story, but the sound of her voice relaxed him and soothed him and made him sleepy. But when the cheerful voices in the house fell silent, and the twins began to breathe deeply as they slept, and the lamp glowed gold in the semi-darkness by his bed, Isaac would cry into the crumpled, white linen handkerchief, until his anguished sobbing became part of his dreams.

*

One bright Saturday, when the blossoms had started appearing on the trees in the village, and the daffodils lined the drive to the big house, Anna Elizabeth stood on the landing helping Lisi dress the cheerful Marta into a new, blue coat. All of a sudden, a deep voice called out in the hall. Anna Elizabeth froze. Father!

In a flash, she turned and ran down the stairs. There he stood. He looked thinner, perhaps, and his eyes were tired, but it was still Father, her darling Father. She flung herself into his arms and found herself sobbing and laughing at the same time, as he held her in his firm embrace. How Anna Elizabeth had missed him.

That evening, Father joined Anna Elizabeth and Isaac as they took Shell out for his evening walk. Anna Elizabeth had not been up to the lookout rock since her experience that wild night, when aggressive planes in the sky had replaced her gentle geese. She felt nervous as she climbed the hill to stand on the jutting piece of rock.

While Isaac explored the hilltop with Shell, Father held her hand as they looked across the lake. Although the sun was low in the sky, the days were lengthening, and spring was very evident. Down in the valley, new-born lambs bleated for their mothers, who in turn called out for them to return from their adventures of the day.

"Life is beautiful Anna Elizabeth," sighed Father.

He stood tall and statuesque on the rock. He took a deep breath and sighed. He tipped his head back as he allowed the last rays of the sun to light his face. As the sun disappeared and the shadows lengthened across the valley, Anna Elizabeth shivered.

"Sometimes things feel dark," said Anna Elizabeth in a small voice as she remembered the nasty night on the hill, and her despised gas mask. She could always confide in Father.

"How do you mean?" he asked, giving her his full attention.

So, Anna Elizabeth told him everything. She talked about all the children and how they needed Mother as much as she did. She told him of her worry that Isaac did not speak at all. She explained how she had to share Shell with Isaac and the other children. And then, she told him of the dark moment on the hill when the geese had disappeared. She was fearful that they would never return.

"Sometimes, since the war began, life seems dark," she repeated. "It does not seem very beautiful."

Father nodded slowly and looked down at the village. His face was sad, and Anna Elizabeth thought his blue eyes seemed full of tears. But then she thought she might have imagined it.

"Do you see those houses Anna Elizabeth?" he asked suddenly.

She nodded.

"As the light fades, some of them seem to be disappearing into the darkness."

Anna Elizabeth could see that he was right. She shivered again as she remembered the mighty monster of her wild memory. Father continued.

"The houses in the valley are being consumed by the

When the Stars Went On

darkness. But, take a moment, and be silent. Just wait," he said.

As they waited, Anna Elizabeth saw first one tiny light shine brightly into the darkness, and then another and another until the whole valley was filled with twinkling lights. The darkness no longer felt oppressive. She looked up at Father and smiled.

"When life seems dark Anna Elizabeth, I need you to remember three things."

Father was speaking seriously, and Anna Elizabeth listened.

"Firstly, always wait for the light. It is usually there somewhere. Give it a chance to appear."

Anna Elizabeth nodded thoughtfully. She knew what he meant.

"Just like the lights in the village," she said, smiling. "We waited and watched, and they appeared."

Father nodded and then went on.

"If the light takes longer than you are willing to wait, then look up. So often, in the darkness, one looks down. Make sure you look up. Sometimes the light is above you."

Anna Elizabeth stared deep into Father's eyes as he spoke.

"And finally, Anna, when the light seems elusive, and you have tried everything," said Father, "then *be* the light."

Anna Elizabeth was not sure she understood. She frowned a little, but at that moment, Shell interrupted their serious discussion and Isaac followed close behind. Father smiled as he ruffled Isaac's hair.

"I think it's supper time, don't you?" he asked.

Isaac nodded, and he and Shell set off down the hill. Father helped Anna Elizabeth down from the lookout rock, and they set off towards the path together.

"Never forget Anna Elizabeth. When the light is elusive, *be* the light!" said Father.

THREE THINGS TO REMEMBER

The next morning when Anna Elizabeth awoke, Father was gone again.

CHAPTER SIX

A SURPRISING DISCOVERY

Everyone missed Father. His kind smile put the children at ease. His strong, but calm personality, filled Eastwood House with a sense of tranquil peace. Anna Elizabeth missed him the most. She knew that he had a very important job. The country needed him. At least, this is what she told herself when she missed him, over and over again.

Early in the spring, the regulation blackout blinds arrived. Both Mother and Father were going to be away. (Mother was going to visit Grandmother in Bexton.) Mr Jenkins, Maisy's father with the fiery red hair, had agreed to oversee the fitting of the blinds. Joseph was a bit put out.

"I can oversee the fitting Mother," he had said as she straightened her hat whilst looking in the hall mirror before leaving for the week in Bexton."You keep treating me as a child. Men my age are off to fight for King and country, but you won't let me oversee this one small thing. I can do it," he insisted.

"I'm sorry you feel that way," said Mrs Eastwood. "I do trust you, Joseph darling, but I would just be happier if Mr Jenkins was helping too. He is so experienced with this sort of thing."

She patted his cheek and then swept out and down the steps to the waiting car. Joseph sighed in frustration. He turned abruptly and went out into the back courtyard, where he found Lisi hanging washing. Anna Elizabeth happened to see them as she passed by one of the upstairs windows.

They stood talking together while Lisi hung the washing.

A SURPRISING DISCOVERY

Anna Elizabeth watched as Joseph ranted to Lisi and paced up and down. At seventeen, Joseph saw himself as the man of the house. He felt frustrated that Mother gave him no credit for what he was doing to help while Father was away. Anna Elizabeth could not hear what Lisi said, but she noticed that Lisi seemed to calm him down. Joseph stopped his pacing. And then, to Anna Elizabeth's great surprise, Lisi looked around furtively, then put her arms around Joseph's neck. She leaned forward and kissed him! Anna Elizabeth ducked away from the window and flopped onto the floor.

"Goodness," she said in surprise to Shell, who stared up at her with interest.

Anna Elizabeth did not say another word. She sat still in stunned astonishment. Lisi and Joseph were secret lovers! No wonder Joseph liked helping out wherever Lisi was. No wonder he appeared now and then with a smile on his face that she had not seen before Lisi had been employed at Eastwood House!

Just then, there was a commotion at the front door, and Shell jumped up with a bark. He ran towards the staircase to go and see who was knocking. The men had arrived to put up the blinds. Mrs Turner showed them in.

"Stupid war," thought Anna Elizabeth for the umpteenth time, echoing the words she had heard Matthew speak.

"I don't want blinds on my windows. Everything keeps changing!"

Forgetting about Lisi and Joseph, she decided to leave the house to Mr Jenkins and the men to put up the blackout blinds. She found Isaac swinging lazily on the swing that hung from one of the big trees near the drive.

"Let's go for a walk to the icehouse," suggested Anna Elizabeth.

Isaac nodded and jumped up happily. He had no idea

what an icehouse was, but he was keen to do anything Anna Elizabeth suggested. With Shell bounding around them excitedly, the children set off on their walk. As they descended the hill on the other side, Anna Elizabeth pointed out the icehouse to Isaac. It was a strange building. Completely built of red brick, it rose out of the ground like a large, round molehill. It had no windows and lay crouched in the shadow of the trees at the bottom of the hill.

"No-one uses it anymore," she said. "Last summer and the summer before that, Matthew, Maisy and I used to play there. It was so nice and cool on the hot July days. We pretended it was our headquarters. Matthew prefers not to play anymore. He has become such a bore. I miss him. He used to think up the best games."

The children reached the icehouse and Isaac tried the door handle.

"Oh, we keep it locked," said Anna Elizabeth. "We keep the key hidden, but Shell always finds it for us. Go on Shell. Find!"

Shell knew exactly what Anna Elizabeth wanted. He immediately started running up and down the drystone wall that ran along the side of the icehouse. Shell sniffed all over the wall until he found a spot that had a small recess. He barked with excitement, wagging his tail. Anna Elizabeth put her hand inside the hollow cavity and pulled out a thin, wooden box.

"Good boy Shell," she said, and Isaac patted him proudly.

She opened the box and showed Isaac the rusty key lying inside. He lifted it out and slid it into the lock of the door. It was surprisingly easy to turn the key. Then Isaac carefully twisted the old door handle and pushed the heavy door inwards. A blast of cold air hit them, and they shivered and giggled.

"Look here," said Anna Elizabeth as they scampered in.

At the far end of the round, brick room, there were three

A SURPRISING DISCOVERY

wooden crates.

"These were our thrones," she said, "and this crate was the table."

In another part of the icehouse lay a jar of stones and two old coats.

"We pretended the stones were nuggets of gold," said Anna Elizabeth "On colder days, we pretended the coats were our furs!"

In the middle of the floor was a pile of sticks and leaves.

"That was our fire," she giggled. "See here, Isaac. Come and sit on the throne. Let's be a knight and lady. Shell can be our faithful horse."

Isaac felt a little bit lost as his grasp of the new language was still not good, but he sat on the crate and pretended to look grand. He did everything Anna Elizabeth asked him to do.

"This is really a very nice place to be," said Anna Elizabeth. "I feel as though it is an escape from home. Sometimes the house is so busy and noisy."

Isaac thought he understood, and he nodded in agreement. Suddenly he noticed Shell sniffing something on the floor. He jumped up and went over to have a look at it. Anna Elizabeth followed.

"Ugh," she gasped. "A cigarette stub. How on earth did that get here?"

Isaac pointed again and again.

"Oh no," squealed Anna Elizabeth. "There are more. This is very strange. Maisy, Matthew and I are the only ones who know where to find the key! We hid it ourselves. Who on earth could have found it? Who has been in here?"

Anna Elizabeth shivered.

"I don't like it," she said. "Someone has been in our icehouse. Let's go!"

Together they pulled the icehouse door closed, and Isaac locked it.

"Let's take the key with us," suggested Anna Elizabeth. "That way, no-one can get inside."

They walked back up the hill, and while they were walking, Anna Elizabeth devised a plan.

"You keep the key," she said conspiratorially. "No one will think you have it."

When they reached Eastwood House, Isaac went straight up to the room he shared with the twins. Thankfully, it was empty, but he had no idea where to hide the key. Then he saw his jacket with the blue embroidered star hanging on the hook on the door. He knew no one would touch that coat. It was as if his coat was an evil entity because of its white and blue armband. Everyone knew what that armband had come to represent over the last few months of the war. Everyone tried to pretend that the coat was not there. Carefully, he reached up and found the inside pocket. Then he silently slipped the wooden box with the icehouse key into the pocket. He felt confident that no one would find it there.

Later that night, for the first time since arriving at Eastwood House, Isaac went to sleep without sobbing into the white handkerchief. He held it to his face, and it comforted him, but he was too busy thinking about the puzzle of who had been in the icehouse. No tears dampened the handkerchief tonight.

Chapter Seven

THE END OF THE FIRST SUMMER

One glorious Saturday morning in August, the children were up early. Excited chatter could be heard throughout the house. The village was holding their annual Summer Fayre, and everyone was going! Isaac had never been to a fayre before. From his silent perch at the top of the stairs, he watched as the girls fussed with helping Lisi pack up the apple pies that Mary, the cook, had made to sell at the fayre. He felt a tremor of excitement in his tummy. The twins came running down the stairs.

"We go to Summer Fayre, we go to Summer Fayre!" Zimeon called happily.

But Anna Elizabeth's brother Joseph caught the boys, as they were about to rush out of the front door.

"Not yet!" he laughed. "First, you must help us carry."

The twins looked at him with big eyes and nodded. Isaac stood up somewhat hesitantly. He would also like to help. Joseph beckoned to him, smiling, and as Isaac joined him, he put out his arm and gave Isaac a rough, kindly wrestle as they all trooped into the kitchen. They collected the large baskets set ready by Mary. Isaac smiled.

The morning passed by in a frenzy of fun, laughter and sunlight. For once, no one gave any thought to the dark emerging war, which was crawling and clawing its way across Europe, like thick, black volcanic lava, destroying everything over which it exploded, gurgled and oozed. Instead, the villagers chose to think only about how much fun they could have in one day!

When the Stars Went On

Maisy Jenkins hugged Anna Elizabeth in delight when she managed to knock a coconut off the coconut shy!

"Well done!" she laughed as Anna Elizabeth claimed her prize.

It was a small, knitted rabbit. Mrs Bray was supporting the war effort by knitting socks for the soldiers, but she had managed to knit toys for prizes using left-over scraps of wool. Anna Elizabeth gave her funny little grey rabbit a hug.

"He is so cute," she giggled.

Shell was sitting next to them, and Maisy knelt to cuddle him.

"Don't worry Shell," she joked, rubbing his silky ears, "you are still Anna's favourite!"

Shell understood, of course, and he looked up at Anna Elizabeth adoringly with his gentle, brown eyes. His pink tongue hung out the side of his mouth, and he seemed to be smiling as he panted in the heat of the summer's day.

Matthew Jenkins joined them, sipping a bottle of home-made ginger ale.

"Let's go and watch the races," he suggested.

"Ooh, yes," agreed the girls.

They set off towards Upper Field, which lay just beyond the village school. There, they found themselves a cool spot in the shade of a large tree, and they settled themselves down to watch a few races.

Boys and girls of all ages had arrived from different villages and towns to compete. Big Andy stood on the track at the starting point, feeling very important. He had been given the task of holding the starting pistol at the beginning of each race. He strutted up and down, waiting for the signal that he was needed. Then he would stand astride the starting line, and hold the pistol high in the air with both hands. Mr Dell from the next village would give a loud shout.

"On your marks, get set…" and Big Andy would fire into the air.

At the sound of the loud crack, the runners would set off at a dash.

"Where is Isaac?" wondered Matthew. "He should run in a race. He is so fast he would win a prize."

But Isaac was nowhere to be seen. He was on the other side of the school by the sugar cake challenge. Strung across the school playground was a long piece of string. Six round, sugar cakes hung from the string. Isaac knew Mary had baked the cakes. She had complained bitterly to him, that because of the war, there were not enough raisins to make them as rich as she preferred. She had given Isaac one to taste from the first batch she had made. He had thought it was delicious.

Now, he was having great fun helping the Good Doctor to string the small, round cakes onto the line. Together, they sold tickets to anyone who wanted to have a go at eating a sweet, sticky, hanging cake, blindfolded! Isaac liked working with the Good Doctor. To his joy, he discovered that the Good Doctor could speak Polish, so Isaac understood all instructions clearly.

The Good Doctor did not seem to notice that Isaac didn't speak a word. As the morning wore on, Isaac found himself smiling at the jokes the Good Doctor made, and once, he almost felt a rumble of laughter begin low in his tummy!

Every year, the fayre ended with a game of Rounders. This year was no exception, and the Good Doctor was in charge of coordinating the village team.

"Would you like to be on my team?" he asked Isaac when there was a lull in cake sales. Isaac had never played Rounders before, so he shook his head.

"Come on," coaxed the Good Doctor. "I will help you."

Isaac looked at him and wrinkled his nose hesitantly. He wished he did not feel so uncertain.

"Come on," said the Good Doctor again, and Isaac, who did not really want to, found himself nodding.

"What? You will?" cried the Good Doctor. "Hooray!"

He cheered and gave Isaac an encouraging pat on the back.

By late afternoon, the fayre was over and had been packed up. All the villagers had gathered under trees and in the shade of the hedges around Upper Field to watch the game.

Lisi and Mary had laid a thick blanket out on the grass. Anna Elizabeth settled herself down beside Kornelia, Gisela and Marta. Zimeon and Jacov came running up to join the happy group. They had been playing football on the other side of the field with lots of other boys. But now, they dispersed to clear space for the game of Rounders. Mother was standing nearby and chatting to Mrs Johnson, the wife of Mr Johnson, the village schoolteacher. (Mrs Johnson had taken over the teaching in the village school when her husband joined the army.) Mother and Mrs Johnson were deep in conversation, but they both turned their heads in surprise when Anna Elizabeth squealed.

"Look! There's Isaac."

CHAPTER EIGHT

ISAAC JOINS IN

Across the field, the Eastwood household could see a large group of people milling about. The Good Doctor was there with a whistle around his neck and a clipboard in his hands. He was discussing something with Mr Donley, who was Big Andy's grandfather. They were the organisers of the game this year, and they were checking over a few final notes before the game began. Hovering close to the Good Doctor, stood a small figure. Isaac! He looked tiny and vulnerable.

"My word," gasped Mother. "Do you think he is on the team?"

All the children jumped up and began calling and waving to Isaac. From way across the field, he heard them, and he lifted a small arm to wave at them. When they saw his wave, they cheered, and they began to chant his name over and over again.

"Isaac, Isaac, Isaac!" they yelled.

The nervous butterflies in Isaac's tummy were making him regret his decision to play. But the supportive cries of his friends sent a warm glow of pride rushing over him. The Good Doctor and Mr Donley began to stride across the field. They were marking out the batting square and setting up the four bases. The players started moving into position and Isaac was lost from view. He was much smaller than the other players and could not be seen.

"There he is," called Maisy who had joined the excited group of children.

When the Stars Went On

She pointed into the distance. The village team were lining up in a rather haphazard line. Isaac had hesitantly taken his place at the back of the line. He looked to the Good Doctor for reassurance and the Good Doctor, who was walking towards the team, smiled and nodded encouragingly.

The captain of each team walked to the centre of the field where they met each other and shook hands. A coin was tossed high into the air to determine who would bat and who would bowl first.

The watching crowd cheered as the village team sent their best bowler in to bowl. The rest of the team, including Isaac, placed themselves around the field. The backstop took his position behind the batsman, and the rest of the team dotted themselves by the posts all around the field. Isaac took the role of one of the three deep fielders.

The first ball was bowled, and as the batsman swung the bat, hitting the ball so that it arced across the blue sky, the crowd gave a loud cheer. The village team raced to catch the ball, and as the game proceeded, it drew many excited yells of delight from the enthusiastic crowd.

Anna Elizabeth kept an eye on Isaac. He seemed so defenceless, and she felt the need to protect him, but she need not have worried. Whilst umpiring, the Good Doctor kept one eye on the game, and one eye on Isaac. He kept bending down to explain things to Isaac, and Isaac seemed to be responding well.

Half time arrived, and the boy scouts from the village ran onto the field carrying tin cups and large, tin buckets filled with cold water. The teams relaxed for a few minutes, chatted to each other, and drank deeply from the tin cups. They had worked up an eager thirst that hot afternoon!

A whistle blew, and the scouts ran off again. The teams were back in position. This time, the village team would be

ISAAC JOINS IN

batting, and the visitors would be bowling and fielding.

The first ball of the second half was bowled, and as it flew across the field, the opposing team ran to catch it. One of the boys on their team was tall, robust, and a fast runner. He raced forward, and with a great leap, he reached up and caught the ball with one hand. The crowd supporting the village team clapped because his action was so well executed, but they groaned at the same time. No points for the village team. What a pity. This meant that the opposing team was already in the lead.

What an exciting afternoon. First, the opposing team had the upper hand, and then, the village team moved ahead. By the end of the afternoon, the village team were lagging behind, 14.5 to 15. They needed their last player to run through all four bases if they were to win the prize that year. Everyone looked to see who the last player was going to be. Isaac! Could he do it? Could Isaac win the game for the village this year?

Nervously, he moved into his position and picked up the wooden bat. He twisted it a few times, then he bent his knees and put the bat over his shoulder as he had seen the other players do.

The tall boy, who was bowling, stared across at Isaac like a warrior staring at his prisoner, and his eyes flashed. Isaac stared back, unperturbed. Then the tall boy began running. His arm swung back and flew under. He let go of the ball, and it streaked across the field in a straight line towards Isaac.

Keeping his eye on the ball, Isaac felt a surge of energy stream through his body. As the ball approached, he swung the bat around.

To his great surprise, he managed to smack the ball powerfully, and it went spiralling up into the air. The crowd began to roar with delight and stood to their feet as the opposing team scrambled to catch the ball. Isaac knew what to do next. Holding onto the bat, he began to run.

The wind caught at his hair, and the sun shone on his face. He recognised the familiar feeling of freedom that came over him when he ran. Then, it was as if the sound of the crowd faded, and the field became nothing but a blur, and Isaac knew his Tata was running beside him.

"Run Isaac. Run," he heard his shining Tata say.

And Isaac ran. Past first base. Past second base. His breathing was fast, but even. His bare feet thudded on the dry grass. Past third base. As he headed for the final base, he heard the crowd roaring.

"Isaac, Isaac, Isaac!" they cried.

And then it was over. The village team had won! The world came rushing back into focus, and Isaac looked around for a second to see Tata, but he was gone. The Good Doctor cheered Isaac as he fell over the last base and tumbled to the ground in a victorious, excited heap.

As Isaac lay on the grass, enjoying the sensation of victory, he felt a wet tongue licking his face. Shell was there sharing in his delight. It seemed to Isaac that the whole village wanted to pat him on the back and tell him how well he had done. The Good Doctor lifted Isaac onto his shoulder, and with the village team following them, they paraded around the field, with Shell barking and bouncing up and down around their feet. Isaac had saved the day! Isaac was the hero of the hour. Isaac lifted his fist into the air, and laughed out loud!

CHAPTER NINE

WHERE IS ZIMEON?

The first summer was followed by a blustery autumn. The rapidly shortening days raced by. When December arrived, the weather had turned grey and icy. Freezing wind cut across the hills and whined over the steel, grey lake. But, inside the small schoolroom in the village, it was warm, and the atmosphere was happy. The excited children were preparing to celebrate Christmas. They were painting pinecones with white, red and green paint. The wooden desks were filled with bits of coloured paper, string and card. Some were colouring pictures of holly and snowmen, whilst others glued long, paper chains.

Mrs Johnson was up on a small ladder in the corner of the classroom. She and some of the older children were setting up a Christmas tree. The smell of pine needles and dusty tinsel filled the room.

"Hand me the lights please, Maisy," she said, stretching her hand downwards.

Maisy, with Isaac helping her, held up the string of coloured lights and Mrs Johnson began to wind them around the tree.

On the other side of the room, Mrs Ellis was helping the younger pupils to make their decorations. Carefully, they cut, glued and sprinkled coloured bits of shiny fabric or white, snowy cotton onto card. The twins, Zimeon and Jakov sat working cheerfully together. Zimeon's cheeks were pink, and his tongue stuck out with effort. Everyone was chattering. Mr Jenkins had brought down his old gramophone, and the children sang along to the scratchy sounds of Christmas music.

When the Stars Went On

There was a happy buzz in the classroom.

The old record that had been turning and turning on the gramophone player ground to a halt as it reached the end of the last song. The classroom plunged into a moment of stillness…

And then, in that quiet moment, Jakov began to sing. It was not a song that anyone recognised. Everyone stopped what they were doing, so that they could listen. He had a pure, clear, lilting voice. He sang as he worked, and everyone listened to the strange words and the misty, haunting tune. They were fascinated.

Suddenly, without warning, Zimeon, who had been sitting quietly beside his twin, stood up. His chair clattered over backwards, and he threw the red and gold card he was cutting onto the floor.

"Stop!" he yelled at his twin furiously. "Stop singing!"

He stood panting, his face red and angry. His rage seemed to slash the atmosphere, and the children jumped with fright. Jakov stared up at him in surprise, his eyes round, his mouth open.

Mrs Johnson, seeing what had happened, hurriedly climbed down from the ladder by the tree and bustled across the room to the sobbing, angry Zimeon.

"There, there," she said soothingly, as she reached him. "What is upsetting you Zimeon?"

"I want him to stop singing," he said furiously, pointing at Jakov. "He must stop singing."

All the children stared at Zimeon, their happy activities forgotten in that dark and distressing moment. They had never seen anyone so angry at school. But he was not finished.

"I hate this!" he screamed.

Bending over, he used his arm to sweep across the table. The coloured paper pieces flew into the air, and as the glue pot

WHERE IS ZIMEON?

fell, it smashed on the floor. The children stared as the sticky, white liquid leaked out and seeped into the scattered paper. Next, they stared at Zimeon with horrified eyes, but he turned and bolted towards the door. Grabbing the handle, he pulled it open and disappeared into the frosty yard.

"Oh, my goodness!" said Mrs Johnson. "Take over for me will you?" she said to Mrs Ellis, who was standing with wide eyes on the other side of the room.

Mrs Johnson hastily followed Zimeon. The children sat, shocked and silent. They had never seen behaviour like this before. They all turned to Mrs Ellis.

"Now then," she said as she began mopping up the glue, "let's get on with our decorations."

But the children were upset.

"Why did he do that?" asked Maisy.

"I don't know," said Anna Elizabeth. "Perhaps Jakov said something to upset him."

"I did not," said Jakov, his voice breaking and tears filling his eyes. "I was only singing. It was a song about lighting candles."

At that moment, the door flew open, and a blast of cold air made the children shiver. Mrs Johnson was back. She closed the door firmly behind her.

"Anna Elizabeth, come here please," she said, walking briskly into her office in the next room.

Anna Elizabeth followed her. Mrs Johnson sat down at her desk and pulled out a piece of paper. She began to write a note very hurriedly.

"Zimeon has run away, Anna, and I cannot find him. He was too quick for me, and he has disappeared. Can you think where he might have gone?"

Anna Elizabeth shook her head.

"No, Mrs Johnson," she said. "He has never done anything like this before."

"In that case, I need you to take this to your mother immediately," said Mrs Johnson, handing Anna Elizabeth the note she had written. "Off you go. I shall go out and look for him again."

Hastily, Anna Elizabeth pulled on her coat, and she wound her scarf around her neck. Without looking back at the class of worried children, she set off with the note. As she ran out into the road, she almost collided with the Good Doctor, who was riding by on his bicycle.

"I'm so sorry," spluttered Anna Elizabeth. "Zimeon has run away, and I must give Mother this note!"

"You say Zimeon is missing?" asked the Good Doctor.

"Yes!" replied Anna Elizabeth shortly. "I'm so sorry. I must go."

She turned away and headed towards the Crinkle Crankle Wall opposite the field leading to the hill near Eastwood House. As she ran, she looked about her, searching all the time for Zimeon. But he was nowhere to be seen. Up the hill she climbed, and barely stopping to catch her breath, she ran down the other side and through the avenue of trees to the big house.

"Mother," she cried as she burst through the front door of Eastwood House.

"Mother, where are you?"

Mrs Eastwood appeared at the top of the stairs, surprised to hear Anna Elizabeth's voice so early in the afternoon. Swiftly, she came down into the hall when she saw the dishevelled child.

"What is it?" she asked worriedly.

Anna Elizabeth held out the note Mrs Johnson had written. "It's Zimeon," she said breathlessly. "He's run away!"

WHERE IS ZIMEON?

Mrs Eastwood stared at the note for a minute, reading it. Then she turned to Mrs Turner, who had come into the hall when she heard the commotion.

"Gather the staff please," said Mrs Eastwood capably. "Zimeon has run away from school. It is very cold outdoors. We must go out and help to find him."

It was not long before Mrs Turner had summoned all the staff, with Gisela and Joseph, to the hall. Mrs Eastwood explained what had happened and asked them all to help search for Zimeon. Everyone agreed, although it was decided that Gisela would stay at home to take care of Marta.

"In any case, it will be better if you are here. Someone should be in the house if Zimeon returns," said Mrs Eastwood.

They were all getting their coats on when there was a knock at the door. It was the Good Doctor with Mr Donley and Mr Jenkins.

"We heard that Zimeon has gone missing," he said. "We thought you might need some assistance."

Mrs Eastwood welcomed them in.

"We were just discussing a plan of action," she said. "We plan to spread out across the hills. Perhaps some of us should spread out through the village."

The three men nodded and Mr Donley, who was part of the Home Guard, handed everyone a whistle.

"If any of you find him, blow on the whistle. That way, we will know that we can call off the search."

Anna Elizabeth had Shell by her side. She listened carefully to the adults.

"May I help?" she asked hopefully, and Shell stood up, wagging his tail.

"No, Anna Elizabeth," said Mrs Eastwood. "You are to stay here where it is warm."

When the Stars Went On

Disappointed, Anna Elizabeth and Shell stood by the long windows in the front room. They watched as the adults spread out across the drive. She could hear their voices as they called out to Zimeon.

"Zimeon," they cried. "Zimeon."

As their calls faded into the distance, Anna Elizabeth sighed. She felt helpless. The sun would soon be disappearing down behind the lake. Zimeon did not know the hills as she did. She sat listening to the clock ticking slowly in the empty, darkening house. Suddenly she heard voices in the hall. The other children had returned from school. Maisy was there too.

"We were told to go home," she told Anna Elizabeth breathlessly. "Mrs Johnson said she needed to search for Zimeon. Isaac and I walked with Jakov to keep him company."

Shortly afterwards, Kornelia arrived home from secondary school and was surprised and shocked to hear the news. Anna Elizabeth told her what had happened.

"Zimeon got upset at school. Jakov was singing, and it seemed to annoy him."

"He just ran out," added Maisy.

"We have no idea where he is. The grown-ups have been searching for ages!" Anna Elizabeth told her.

"What song were you singing?" asked Kornelia turning to Jakov. "Sing it for me."

Jakov cleared his throat and in a shaky voice, began to sing it for her. She recognised it at once and began to sing along.

"Oh yes," she said, nodding her head. "I know the song well. It is a song we sing at Hanukkah."

Anna Elizabeth and Maisy looked puzzled, so she continued.

"Hanukkah is a celebration. We used to celebrate Hanukkah every year. It is a little bit like Christmas because we had decorations and nice food and sometimes presents too."

WHERE IS ZIMEON?

Isaac, who was listening silently, smiled and nodded as Kornelia and Jakov described the Hanukkah celebrations they remembered.

"We had a menorah," said Jakov, his face shining. "It had nine candles."

"We lit two on the first night, and then an extra one every night after that," explained Kornelia. "The celebration lasted eight days."

Gisela, who had put Marta down to nap, joined everyone in the front room.

"I miss Hanukkah," she said sadly. "I miss the time we spent with our family. It was always so joyful."

There was silence as the children sat remembering. Maisy stared at their troubled faces. She spoke softly.

"Do you think it was the song that made Zimeon sad? Perhaps the decorations and the music made him remember things he does not have anymore."

Anna Elizabeth nodded thoughtfully. She looked at the children who suddenly seemed more lost and sad than she had ever seen them.

Abruptly, she stood up. It was time to take Shell for his evening walk. While Anna Elizabeth pulled on her boots and a warm coat, she wondered what she could do to help the children. They all looked so forlorn. The fact that Zimeon was still missing terrified her. She clipped Shell's lead on and together they left Eastwood House by the back door. Anna Elizabeth decided to walk through the kitchen garden for a change. Making her way along the frosty stone paths, she found herself thinking about Zimeon and his outburst of anger when he heard a song from his past. She could not even begin to imagine his sadness and his longing.

Anna Elizabeth and Shell headed towards the gate in the

tall wall at the end of the garden. A small, rickety shed stood by the ornate, iron gate. As they neared the shed at the end of the garden, Shell suddenly began to pull on his lead. Anna Elizabeth pulled him back onto the path.

"Stop that, Shell," she said sternly.

But Shell pulled again at his lead, and whined.

"What is it, Shell?" she exclaimed. "Why are you pulling me?"

As she strained to pull him closer to the gate, Shell began to fight against walking with her. He battled wildly, trying to free himself from the lead. She had never seen him behave in such a manner. His disobedience was most unusual. She stopped pulling him, and he wagged his tail, edging towards the shed. Anna Elizabeth decided to follow him. Perhaps Shell was trying to show her something. At the shed door, he sniffed and whined, wagging his tail. He lifted his paw and scratched the door. Anna Elizabeth was puzzled. She decided to open the door of the shed. Shell gave a small bark and immediately rushed inside. Anna Elizabeth peered around the door into the dark, gloomy space filled with equipment used for gardening.

"Have you found a rat again?" she asked Shell nervously.

In the corner, she could just make out a pile of dirty, old sacks. Suddenly she squealed in fright, for the sacks were moving! Anna Elizabeth stared in horror as a thin, pale hand pushed back the pile of grubby bags. A dirty, streaked face appeared like a ghostly, mournful apparition in the darkness. She jumped backwards, but Shell was not afraid. He scrabbled up onto the pile of sacks and began to lick the frightened little face.

"Zimeon!" Anna Elizabeth cried in relief.

Chapter Ten

A NEW CELEBRATION

Anna Elizabeth stepped into the shed and crouched down beside the pile of sacks with Zimeon.

"There you are. We have been so worried about you," she said anxiously. "Are you alright?"

But Zimeon was still angry.

"Leave me!" he said, his black eyes flashing in the darkness.

It did not seem to matter how kind Anna Elizabeth was to him, or how much she coaxed and pleaded, Zimeon was not going to return with her to Eastwood House. For the second time that day, Anna Elizabeth felt utterly helpless. She stood up, feeling defeated. She would have to go back and find an adult to help her.

"It's cold. I have to go back," she said shortly. "Come on, Shell."

But Shell had his own ideas. He lay down beside Zimeon and refused to move, no matter how much Anna Elizabeth cajoled and pulled on his lead. By now, it was very dark, and the cold was bitter.

"Please Zimeon," begged Anna Elizabeth again.

Her teeth were beginning to chatter as the icy air penetrated her coat.

"Please come. If you don't, Shell will stay here, and you will both freeze. It is much too cold out here."

Zimeon peered down in the darkness, trying to see Shell lying beside him. He put his cold hand onto Shell's head and stroked his black, silky ears. They felt cold to touch.

"I come with you," he suddenly said abruptly. "I come. I not want Shell to be cold."

Anna Elizabeth breathed a sigh of relief, and she put her hand out to help Zimeon extricate himself from the muddy sacks. He refused to take her hand, but he took Shell's lead as together they made their way back to the house. Every now and then, Shell would give Zimeon's icy fingers a quick, encouraging lick.

Back inside the warm house, the waiting children rushed over to Zimeon, but he ignored them. He ran upstairs and shut himself in his room.

"Leave him," said Anna Elizabeth. "Mother will know what to do."

Gisela went out onto the drive at the front of the house and she blew the whistle she had been given. It's shrill screech echoed with a piercing cry around and around the black hills. Soon, the adults out searching for Zimeon, began to arrive back at the house, their lamps bobbing in the frosty darkness.

Mrs Eastwood looked grey with cold and worry.

"He is in his room," Anna Elizabeth informed her. "He won't talk to any of us."

Mrs Eastwood, Lisi and the Good Doctor went up the stairs to find Zimeon, and Mr Jenkins called to Maisy.

"Come on, young lady. Let's get you home again."

Mrs Turner spoke to the rest of the children.

"It's time for bed," she said. "Isaac and Jakov, I'll make up a bed for you in the study."

In the warm darkness of her room, Anna Elizabeth lay awake for a long time that night. She could not shake the troublesome sense of helplessness in her heart. She could not forget the cold fury in Zimeon's eyes as he struggled to come to terms with his new life away from his family. Deep into the night, she lay wondering what Mother and the Good Doctor were saying to Zimeon. As she lay thinking, an idea began to form in her head. Feeling happier, she drifted off to sleep.

The next morning, all the children gathered around the breakfast table. Zimeon was not there. He arrived shortly after Mrs Turner served the children their porridge. He held the hand of Mrs Eastwood, who had brought him in, but he kept his eyes down.

"Zimeon has something to say to you all," said Mrs Eastwood.

Keeping his eyes down, Zimeon spoke softly.

"I am sorry," he said. "I was sad, but I was wrong to make you worry."

All the children stared at him silently, feeling uncomfortable. The ever-forgiving Shell, however, walked over to Zimeon wagging his tail. He was not allowed to leap up against anyone, but today he disobeyed his house rules and jumped up onto the ashamed, small boy. Surprised, Zimeon fell over backwards and landed on his bottom with a bump! It broke the sense of discomfort in the room, and everyone burst into laughter.

Jumping up, they all gathered about Zimeon hugging him and laughing, and telling him all at once about how they had missed him. Shell was delighted. Wagging his tail so that his whole body wriggled from side to side, he seemed to be smiling as he ambled about the happy children, licking whatever leg or hand he could reach. Anna Elizabeth stretched out an arm to help Zimeon up, and this time he took her hand, giving her a wry smile as he did so.

As they sat down to continue with their breakfast, Anna Elizabeth spoke.

"I have an idea," she said excitedly. "Let's plan a Hanukkah celebration. We could have it here in the dining room."

For a moment, everyone sat in silent surprise, taking in her idea. Then Isaac smiled and nodded.

"We will need a menorah," said Jakov in a small voice.

"I have one," said Lisi, who had walked into the room with a pot of tea.

Everyone stared at her in surprise.

"I brought it with me when I came to England from Poland," she explained. "My Grandmother insisted. You may borrow it."

"We could invite the Good Doctor," said Mrs Eastwood, smiling.

"And Maisy," exclaimed Anna Elizabeth.

Pushing her chair back from the table, she ran to collect a pencil and paper.

"Come on," she urged, as the children and Lisi gathered around her excitedly. "I shall write down your ideas for the celebration."

*

Eight days before the end of the term, the family celebrated Hanukkah. Mrs Turner, the housekeeper, did her best to plan meals even though rationing made it difficult to find the required special ingredients. Gisela and Kornelia taught Mary how to make 'latkes' using potatoes from the garden.

"We always eat latkes at Hanukkah," explained Kornelia. "We grate the potato and add egg and special flour."

Fried in butter, they were a delicious addition to the celebration meal.

Every evening after school, for the eight days of Hanukkah, the children came home to find the dining room ready for a few hours of togetherness and celebration. Mrs Turner outdid herself, bringing out the silverware and the best white linen tablecloth, usually reserved for Christmas. Mrs Eastwood cut long branches of green rosemary, which she tied together with a blue, silk ribbon before placing it in a crystal vase on the dark wood sideboard. Every evening the Good Doctor came and led evening prayers before supper. This was always followed by party games or stories planned by Lisi and Joseph.

But most beautiful in the eyes of the six Jewish children, was the shining, silver menorah. Each night, as the shadows of nightfall fell heavily on Eastwood house, and the curtains were drawn against the cold frostiness of the night, the Good Doctor lit first two, then three, then four candles, until all the candles were shining, and illuminating the faces of the friends gathered around the table.

On the last night of Hanukkah, Zimeon stood up. The glowing candles lit his face, and his eyes were shining. He was wearing a clean, white shirt and his short hair had been combed flat. He had borrowed a tie from Joseph, and he suddenly looked very grown-up as he rapped on the table to get everyone's attention.

"Please," he said. "I wish to speak."

Everyone fell silent as they turned to look at Zimeon.

"I wish, first, to thank *you*," he said, turning to Mrs Eastwood.

Everyone clapped. But Zimeon held up his hand.

"I wish to thank Good Doctor too," he said. "And also, I want to thank everyone here for making beautiful Hannukah for us. It has made me so very happy."

Everyone clapped and cheered again, but Zimeon was not finished. He held up his hand again.

"Please," he repeated, "I wish to do one more thing. He turned to his twin. "Will you help me?"

When the Stars Went On

Jakov stood up and moved to stand beside Zimeon. Everyone waited expectantly, wondering what was going to happen.

To everyone's surprise, Zimeon began to sing. His small, clear voice rang out into the room. Turning to Jakov, he nodded his head, and Jakov joined his brother, their small voices blending as one. United by the very music that had made Zimeon so angry, they now sang the song they remembered from their lives in Poland; a song that they had last sung for Hanukkah when they were with their families. It was a time they remembered with longing and sadness, but it was a time they wanted to share with their new friends. As their voices rang out, Lisi, Gisela, Kornelia and the Good Doctor joined them.

Mrs Eastwood wiped a small tear from the corner of her eye. Isaac, of course, was not able to sing along, but he stood near them shyly, one hand stroking Shell. Anna Elizabeth could see he was mouthing the words of the song to himself:

> *'The candles are burning low,*
> *one for each night.*
> *To remind us of days long ago,*
> *they shed a sweet light.*

CHAPTER ELEVEN

WHEN THE STARS WENT ON

More than a year had passed since the Kindertransport had brought the six children from Poland to Eastwood House. Marta was growing fast and by the end of next year, would be joining the infants at the village school. She rarely cried for her Mama anymore. Gisela no longer looked thin and exhausted, and she enjoyed the lessons that she had with Mrs Eastwood. Together they pored over atlases, books of history, poetry, and English grammar. Gisela loved learning and could not get enough of it. She read in every spare moment she had.

With time, Kornelia had settled and had become less bossy and argumentative. She had given up trying to make Isaac speak. Instead, she busied herself helping Lisi with sewing and mending. She was good at darning socks, and Lisi had promised her that one day, she would teach her how to knit. Zimeon and Jacov were cheerful and helpful, and they adored Joseph, who let them help him with all sorts of jobs around the house and garden. The family, like many other families in the village, now had a pig out in the back yard. Lisi was afraid of the pig, and so Joseph and the twins took on the responsibility of feeding it all the scraps that Mary threw out each day.

Anna Elizabeth and Isaac had become firm friends, and they both took care of Shell, taking him for long walks in the hills. Sometimes planes flew overhead, and while they scared Anna Elizabeth so that she would hug Shell, burying her head in his soft fur until they had passed over, Isaac stared up at them defiantly.

When the Stars Went On

One terrible day, Anna Elizabeth and Isaac were out on the hills, when they heard a high-pitched whining in the sky. They looked up to see what could be making the eerie shriek. To their horror, they saw a plane high above them burst into flames. They watched as it began to spiral downwards, spinning helplessly, erratically, and leaving a black smoke trail in the sky. They lost sight of it as it rattled and bawled blindly down, behind the dark trees on the hillside.

After that, there was lots of talk in the village about a German plane that had crashed in a nearby field. Matthew told Anna Elizabeth that he had overheard his father talking to Big Andy and Mr Donley.

"Apparently," said Matthew, "they haven't found the pilot of the plane. They think he might have survived the crash and could be hiding somewhere near the village. Everyone has been told to keep an eye out for him, and to take care."

Anna Elizabeth did not like this. From then on, she tried to make sure they took Shell out for walks in the daylight. She missed her evening walks, but she was terrified of bumping into the German soldier in the dark.

"Whatever would we say to him?" she asked Isaac.

But of course, Isaac did not answer.

January brought snow showers across the village and surrounding hills. It also brought Joseph's eighteenth birthday. The family met in the parlour early one afternoon, to celebrate. A warm fire glowed in the grate, and on the table stood a large cake. Mary had baked the cake using eggs the twins had collected. Lisi decorated it with a thin blue ribbon she had saved from when she had made a new dress the previous year. Anna Elizabeth noticed that Lisi was wearing the pretty dress that she had made, and she saw how pleased she looked when Joseph gave her a secret smile of admiration.

WHEN THE STARS WENT ON

Nobody else saw their eyes lock, because Mrs Turner came into the room looking flustered and shaking her head.

"Well, how about that!" she exclaimed. "It seems I have mislaid the silver cake forks and serving platter."

Mrs Eastwood looked up sharply.

"Whatever do you mean Mrs Turner?" she asked.

"Well, said Mrs Turner thinking carefully, "the last time I saw them was at Christmas time. We had them out on Christmas day. I always keep them in the drawer by the pantry, but they are not there."

She looked perplexed.

"I'll help you look for them later," said Mary helpfully. "I'm sure we will find them somewhere."

They all tucked into the cake and assured Mary that it was the most delicious cake they had ever tasted. They all knew she had struggled to make it with less butter and sugar than usual, because of rationing. But poor Mary hardly noticed their kind remarks. She was worried about the silverware that was missing and could not wait to get back to the kitchen to search for it. She was also worried because the more she thought about it, the more she thought other things were missing from the kitchen too. Mary was sure she had had a few more apples left over in the pantry, but when she had wanted to make an apple pie, she had been surprised to see how few apples were left. And, the matches were definitely missing. Mary was feeling vexed.

Because of the afternoon celebrations with Joseph, it was quite late before Anna Elizabeth and Isaac were able to take Shell for his evening walk. A light dusting of snow lay across the fields, and it was very cold, but the sky was clear. They set off through the avenue of trees, and turned to climb the hill. At the top, they chose to run down in the direction of the village.

Before they knew it, they found themselves heading towards the icehouse. Anna Elizabeth stopped.

"I don't want to go there," she said fearfully.

But Isaac frowned and continued walking. He was not scared, and he wanted to see if there were any more clues about who might have been visiting the icehouse.

He had often thought about the peculiar building and the cigarette stubs that had worried Anna Elizabeth. Besides, Anna Elizabeth had involved him in the mystery by giving him the key to keep hidden. Every night, after the twins were asleep, Isaac checked that it was still in the pocket of his jacket, and each night he wondered who had been in the icehouse. So, this evening, he was eager to find out if he could see anything that might tell him more. Shell pulled on his lead, wanting to follow Isaac. So Anna Elizabeth moved forward. Slowly. They trudged across the snowy field, and Isaac walked right up to the icehouse. Anna Elizabeth, feeling cautious, stayed further back.

As Isaac drew near, he saw something that made his heart beat faster. He could see that there were footprints in the frozen mud around the door of the icehouse. He knelt to examine them more closely. They were large footprints, and he wondered whose they could be. It looked as though good, durable boots had made the prints. Big Andy had sturdy boots. Could it be that Big Andy sometimes came to the icehouse?

Standing up, Isaac examined the lock of the door, and his heart skipped a beat. There were scratch marks around the lock. He was sure they had not been there before. Someone had tried to tamper with the lock! He twisted the handle, but the door remained closed. Whoever had tried to pick the lock had not succeeded in opening the icehouse. Isaac walked around to the other side of the house. His sharp eyes spotted another cigarette stub. Somebody was definitely hanging around the place. Isaac decided not to gesture to Anna Elizabeth to call her over. He did not want to point out the suspicious things he had noticed. It would only make her uneasy. Isaac knew she was already anxious about noisy planes and gas masks. She did not need to be scared of anything else.

He turned and walked back to Anna Elizabeth. Then, he beckoned to her to follow him, and they made their way back up the powdery, white hill. Although it was bitterly cold and getting dark, Anna Elizabeth could not resist taking a moment to enjoy the view of the village nestled by the silver lake. Together they stood and watched as the sun, already hidden from view, made a deep crimson stripe between the earth and the sky.

Then, the fiery, red stripe was gone. The children watched as the village below sank into gloomy obscurity as the last red light faded. Anna Elizabeth found herself waiting for the lights of the village to start twinkling, but then she remembered that all the cottages now had blackout blinds. Her heart sank.

"Stupid war!" she said. "The blackout blinds have taken away the lights of the village. I miss their shine. They were always so comforting."

For a long moment, Anna Elizabeth and Isaac stared down into the darkness, contemplating the loss of the village lights. But Isaac shifted his gaze so that he could look up into the clear, night sky.

Then something remarkable happened…

Isaac spoke!

"Anna," he said clearly.

Her name did not stick in his throat. She turned at the sound of his voice and stared incredulously, her eyes and mouth wide open in surprise.

"Anna," he said again, his eyes turned heavenward. "Look

up."

But Anna Elizabeth could not take her eyes off him. Isaac was speaking.

"Anna, look up!"

He spoke with an urgency that she could not ignore. Dragging her eyes from his face, she tilted her head and looked up. As far as she could see, the sky was filled with tiny, twinkling stars; a million glittering diamonds in a dark dome.

"Oh," she whispered breathlessly. "Oh, I've never seen so many stars!"

And then, she understood. For so long, the bright lights of the village had hidden the splendour of the Milky Way from her. But now, thanks to those blackout blinds, a whole new beauty had revealed itself to Anna Elizabeth. Father had been right. All she had needed to do to find relief from the darkness, was to look up! Isaac smiled across at her. And then, not faltering at all, he spoke smoothly, and confidently, with no choking and with no struggle.

"The lights went out. The stars went on."

CHAPTER TWELVE

A TELEGRAM ARRIVES

It did not seem long before the summer returned, and the children once again delighted in the long, warm days. They helped old Mr Briggs, the gardener, in the herb and vegetable garden, which he was now extending. Mother had decided more of their land should be used for growing food to share with the villagers. So, Mr Briggs spent many hours plotting out the new vegetable garden. Assisted by Mr Jenkins, they turned over the soil with picks and forks. Mrs Ellis, the help teacher, whose husband was away at war, brought in cartloads of manure from their farm. The children joked that the big house had turned into a stable, because the odour of the manure permeated every room in the house!

Anna Elizabeth, Kornelia and Gisela all helped to plant out seedlings. Anna Elizabeth loved fingering the tiny plants with baby tendrils. She enjoyed gently placing them in the soil, knowing that with care and nurturing, the plants would provide food for them all through the winter. Every day the twins helped to water the baby plants, and Anna Elizabeth watched as the seedlings grew and stretched their tiny leaves to the sun.

Isaac was sent on all kinds of errands. Mrs Eastwood often asked him to deliver spare needles to Mrs Bray for her knitting, or a vase to the ladies planning the next flower festival in the church.

"He runs so fast, it would be pointless to take the car to the village and back," smiled Mother.

When the Stars Went On

One Saturday morning, after planting baby carrots for an hour in the hot sun, the girls stood up to ease their aching backs. They were in need of a break. As they poured themselves a cup of cold water from the jug provided by Lisi, Kornelia spoke.

"I wish every day be like this."

Gisela and Anna Elizabeth nodded. The war seemed far away today. Birds chattered in the trees above them, and the sky was clear and blue. Almost no planes had roared overhead, and that was an enormous relief to Anna Elizabeth. She hated it when squadrons of planes rumbled over Eastwood House. But mostly, she hated it when the Home Guard sent out urgent warnings, and the desperate sound of whistles rang out across the village and echoed around and around the valley. Then everyone would run down into the dark, damp cellar of the house. There, they would stay until someone told them it was safe to come out. But today, she did not need to think about that. Kornelia continued.

"I not want to go to school anymore," she said looking down at her feet. "The children no like me and I fright of Big Andy."

Anna Elizabeth could not help feeling that Kornelia deserved to feel that none of the children liked her. Kornelia was not always a very likeable person. She immediately felt guilty for thinking this thought, so she turned to Kornelia.

"Never mind. The summer holidays are only weeks away. Perhaps things will feel better after that."

But Kornelia was persistent.

"Big Andy make me fright," she insisted haltingly. "He say he want to be a soldier. He say he want to fight."

Anna Elizabeth rolled her eyes and shrugged.

"Big Andy is always boasting about his strength," she said, "but he only ever uses it to tackle an opposing team when he plays rugby."

A TELEGRAM ARRIVES

"But, Big Andy say he fight anything not good," said Kornelia, tears welling up in her eyes. "He say it to me." Her face crumpled as she began to cry. "He think I am not good."

"Oh dear," said Anna Elizabeth. "I feel sure that you misunderstood what he meant."

Anna Elizabeth was not fond of Kornelia, but if what she was saying was true, then Big Andy's behaviour was not acceptable. Nevertheless, she was confident that Big Andy was not deliberately trying to be nasty to Kornelia. Gisela too, had listened to what Kornelia had said.

"Perhaps you tell Mrs Eastwood," she suggested kindly.

"Yes," said Anna Elizabeth. "I will go with you. She will know what to do."

"I tell Mrs Eastwood tonight," said Kornelia resolutely as she put down her cup. She wiped her eyes with the back of her sleeve. For the first time, Anna Elizabeth felt sorry for Kornelia, who sniffed, and bravely went back to digging a small trench for the carrots.

Anna Elizabeth was secretly unnerved by what Kornelia had told her that morning. She felt cross with Big Andy. He was always boasting, and all he wanted to do was to be a soldier and a hero, but he was not old enough! Anna Elizabeth resolved to tell Mother as soon as she could. But all thought of Big Andy was driven from her head by some news brought to them by Maisy.

Just before dinner time, as the girls were washing their faces and hands, and brushing their hair, there was a knock on the front door. It seemed to echo ominously through the house, and Anna Elizabeth wondered who it could be. She quickly tucked the last unruly curls behind her ears, and ran downstairs to see who might be visiting at such an hour. Dinnertime was not usually interrupted by visitors.

When the Stars Went On

Lisi opened the door. Maisy stood on the threshold looking small and scared, her fiery, red hair dishevelled, and her face hot and streaked with sweat. Anna Elizabeth ran towards her, concerned.

"Maisy!" she exclaimed. "Whatever is the matter?"

Maisy held out her hand. She was holding an envelope with a note inside.

"It's for Mrs Eastwood," she said breathlessly.

Lisi took the note and went upstairs to find Mrs Eastwood, who had not yet arrived in the dining room for dinner.

Anna Elizabeth took Maisy into the kitchen.

"Come and get some water to drink," she said to Maisy.

She pulled out a chair by the table. Maisy sat down, and gulped the cool water. Anna Elizabeth sat, watching and waiting to hear what news Maisy had to share with her.

Maisy finished her cold drink and sat back in her seat. She looked at Anna Elizabeth seriously.

"I think something bad has happened," she said in a straight voice, "but I can't be sure."

"Why?" said Anna Elizabeth. "What do you know?"

"Well," said Maisy, "I was down at Mrs Bray's house. I go there most days to help her feed the chickens, and to clean the cages."

Anna Elizabeth nodded. She knew Maisy liked to help out at Mrs Bray's, and Mrs Bray loved having the bright, friendly Maisy to chat to each day.

"Well," continued Maisy, "I was crouched behind the wall, cleaning the water bowl for the chickens, but I stood up just in time to see a telegraph boy racing by on his bike. I wondered where he was going."

Anna Elizabeth leaned forward, listening carefully.

"I decided to collect the eggs next," said Maisy. "There were

A TELEGRAM ARRIVES

quite a few, so it took me a while. When I had found all the eggs, I took them inside to Mrs Bray. She and the Good Doctor were just about to make tea, so I stood talking a while. Then, I went back out to finish cleaning the coop. I had just walked out to the garden when I saw my mother walking up the street with the telegraph boy. He was walking beside her, pushing his bike."

Anna Elizabeth held her breath in surprise.

"They stopped outside Mrs Johnson's front gate, which, of course, is right opposite Mrs Bray's cottage. They talked for a few seconds," said Maisy, "and then they opened the gate and went up to the front door."

By this time, Mary, who had been about to serve dinner, was also listening to Maisy. She stood by the table with her hands on her hips, engrossed in the telling of the tale.

"They knocked at the door, and I saw Mrs Johnson open it. The telegraph boy handed her an envelope. Mrs Johnson took one look and put her hand to her mouth. Then she and Mother went inside, closing the door behind them. The telegraph boy got back onto his bike and rode away."

"It'll not be good news," said Mary in a gloomy voice as she folded her arms resolutely.

"Go on!" said Anna Elizabeth to Maisy urgently.

"There is not much more to tell," said Maisy, "except that Mama came running over the street to call the Good Doctor. And then, when she saw me, she asked Mrs Bray for a piece of paper and an envelope. She quickly wrote a note and asked me to bring it here."

At that moment, Mrs Eastwood, walked briskly into the kitchen, interrupting Maisy's story.

"Mary," she said brusquely.

"Yes, Ma'm?" enquired Mary, standing politely to attention.

When the Stars Went On

"Please could you serve dinner to the children at once, but please make sure to save some for me. I have been called to Mrs Johnson's house, and I shall not have time to eat now."

Lisi had followed her into the kitchen.

"Lisi, please make sure that the children do their chores this afternoon. I have no idea how long I will be gone."

Lisi nodded obediently, and with that, Mother swept out of the house. She got into a car, which was already waiting for her in the drive.

Everyone fell silent. Everyone was sure they knew what Mrs Johnson had read in the telegram.

*

The children did not see Mrs Eastwood again until the next morning. Lisi brought a message to the breakfast table to say that the children were required to meet Mrs Eastwood in Father's study. Anna Elizabeth was surprised. They very rarely went into the study without Father.

Nevertheless, as soon as breakfast was over, Lisi took little Marta to play in the garden. The other children all trooped into the study. Mother was sitting behind Father's large desk. She was writing a letter. The children lined up on the opposite side of the desk, and Mother put down her pen. She looked up and smiled at them, although her eyes remained serious. Anna Elizabeth thought she looked pale and tired.

"I am afraid I have some sad news," began Mrs Eastwood. "You probably have all guessed that the telegram received by Mrs Johnson did not bring good news. In fact, the telegram was to inform Mrs Johnson that Mr Johnson has been killed in battle."

The children remained silent. They were shocked, and not

A TELEGRAM ARRIVES

sure what to say.

"I am sorry to have to tell you this, but it does affect you because both Mr and Mrs Johnson were responsible for your education as your teachers. And, of course, Mrs Johnson is my friend."

Mrs Eastwood's voice broke, and she stood up quickly to stand at the window with her back to the children. After a moment, she continued.

"Obviously, this means that those of you attending the village school will not be able to go back until we have made some plans. In the meantime, I will need you to study here at home, until such time that Mrs Johnson feels she can return to school, if at all."

Kornelia sniffed.

"Poor Mrs Johnson," she said. "She must be so sad!"

"She is," said Mrs Eastwood shortly.

Tentatively, the children began to ask Mrs Eastwood questions, but Anna Elizabeth could not hear what they were saying.

"Stupid war," she said silently in her head. "Stupid, stupid war."

Isaac glanced at her. Nothing on her face showed that she had been affected by the news except that her eyes, fixed unseeingly on the desk, were smouldering. Her lips were pressed together in a thin line and her usually rosy face looked grey. Shell jumped up and pawed her hand. Shell understood. He had sensed a quickening of her breathing, and he knew her heart was pounding. Anna Elizabeth turned abruptly. She needed some time alone. She needed air. She needed to take Shell, and escape from the oppressive atmosphere. Out in the hall she grabbed his lead and headed for the hills.

CHAPTER THIRTEEN

BEING THE LIGHT

It was as if a cloud had descended on Eastwood House. There were no longer happy shrieks as the children prepared to set off to school in the morning. Instead, as they gathered together to study under the guidance of Mrs Eastwood and Lisi, they were reminded with every loud tick of the old clock in the dining room, that they were not at school! It reminded them that Mr Johnson would not be returning to that happy place of learning. Only Marta, who did not understand, kept smiling and laughing.

To make matters worse, news came from the village that a thief was about. Many of the villagers were complaining that their belongings were going missing. So, to add to their troubles, everyone had to keep doors and windows firmly locked. Mrs Bray said that her crystal vase had disappeared from her front window where she always kept it, filled with flowers. Big Andy, who was always trying to impress Kornelia with his tales, told her that the bread his Grandmother had made had been stolen from its cooling tray by the back door.

"It's that missing pilot," said Big Andy in his booming voice. "Mark my words. It's that blooming missing pilot who crashed his plane nearby."

But when Anna Elizabeth and Isaac heard old Mr Trot complaining that there were cigarette stubs around the churchyard, their blood ran cold! They stared at each other, both thinking about the cigarette stubs in the icehouse. Was the lost pilot the village thief? Could he be using the icehouse as a place to hide? Had he been smoking his cigarettes in the icehouse? Anna Elizabeth was worried. Isaac kept thinking that he should investigate the footprints around the icehouse a bit more.

One morning, Anna Elizabeth came downstairs early. She was looking forward to having a walk with Shell before lessons began. She loved making her way across the hills while they were still fresh and damp with dew. As she came downstairs, she heard angry voices. She stopped in surprise. This was most unusual. Anna Elizabeth could not remember ever hearing voices raised in anger in Eastwood House. As she made her way into the large hall, she realised that the sounds she could hear, came from Father's study. The door was slightly ajar.

"You don't need me here, Mother," a voice said heatedly.

Anna Elizabeth realised it was Joseph, talking to Mother. She stopped outside the study door, not wishing to eavesdrop, but not wanting to walk away when she could hear that Mother and Joseph were upset.

"Of course, we need you here," said Mrs Eastwood. "The whole village relies on us, our family, to keep things ticking over. Your father is away, and who knows when he will be back? I know you think I don't appreciate you, but I cannot do this alone Joseph."

"Oh, don't be so dramatic," said Joseph rudely.

Anna Elizabeth was shocked. Never could she have imagined Joseph speaking to Mother in such a disrespectful way. He went on.

"The village has any number of men to support them."

He began to list them.

"Mr Jenkins, Mr Donley..."

"Don't be absurd, Joseph," retorted Mother. "You know what I mean. We have some standing in the village, some financial credibility, and people look to us for help."

"That is what you like to think, Mother," said Joseph. "The truth is that people can manage without you."

"I could say the same about you and the army then," said Mrs Eastwood.

"Well, I'm going anyway," said Joseph stubbornly. "I'm leaving on the nine o'clock bus!"

Anna Elizabeth heard Mrs Eastwood gasp with horror.

"You and your charity," continued Joseph furiously. "Not everyone needs you even though you like to think that. Except of course for the Good Doctor who apparently thinks that you and Father should be helping the whole world."

"Joseph," cried Mrs Eastwood shocked. "You know exactly why the doctor needs us. For goodness sake, he is here for the same reason as these blessed children and your beloved Lisi. If it hadn't been for your father helping them..." she broke off, not wanting to say any more.

Joseph must have looked at her sharply because she continued.

"Oh, yes! Don't think I haven't seen you and Lisi with your secret smiles."

Anna Elizabeth could not stand it anymore. She burst into the study.

"Stop it. Stop it," she cried.

Both Mrs Eastwood and Joseph turned to face her. She was bristling with fury. But the sight of Joseph shocked Anna Elizabeth beyond anything she could have thought of before.

Joseph was dressed in uniform. Joseph was going to war!

"She wasn't supposed to find out like this," Joseph groaned, glaring at his mother.

He turned and left the room. Mrs Eastwood sank down in Father's chair behind the desk. For a moment, Anna Elizabeth stared at her, and for the second time that week, the air in the study stifled her. She needed to get out.

"Come, Shell," she muttered.

She left the house, and the large wooden door closed wearily behind her as she ran down the stone steps.

Out on the hill, as always, she found that she began to relax and her distressed, racing heart began to slow down. She trudged on, up and up. Trapped deep in dark thoughts, she did not see much of her surroundings. She kept her eyes on the rough path, so as not to trip. She was intent on reaching the lookout rock. She needed to stare across the village to the lake. With a bit of luck, she might even see the geese. As she drew near to the lookout rock, she looked up. Someone was sitting there.

She froze for a second. Who was it? Who was trespassing on their land? Was it the lost German pilot? At that moment, the figure moved, and Anna Elizabeth could see that it was Mrs Johnson. She breathed a sigh of relief. She had no need to be afraid of her.

Mrs Johnson had not seen Anna Elizabeth, and she was not sure she wanted to be seen. She had no idea what one said to someone who had received such a sad telegram.

But Shell had other ideas. Pulling on his lead, he broke free and scampered up to Mrs Johnson wagging his tail. Anna Elizabeth watched as Mrs Johnson turned, crouched down, and put both arms around him. Shell licked her face. Then, she looked at Anna Elizabeth, who began to walk hesitantly up to Mrs Johnson.

"Hello Anna," said Mrs Johnson standing up.

Anna Elizabeth could see Mrs Johnson had been crying and she had no idea what to say. This was her teacher, her smiling, happy, clever, interesting teacher, who now looked lost, lonely and vulnerable. It made Anna Elizabeth feel uncomfortable.

When the Stars Went On

She looked at the ground and kicked a small stone. Then she noticed a little white flower growing in a clump of grass between two dark rocks. Bending down, she picked it, and hesitantly held it out to Mrs Johnson.

There they stood, out on the dew-kissed hill above the silver lake, a widow and a girl, a black dog and a snow-white flower.

Mrs Johnson broke the silence.

"Thank you, Anna. How beautiful," she said softly, as she took the delicate flower. A small smile broke across the shadows in her face.

At that moment, it was as if Anna Elizabeth could hear Father speaking to her.

"Be the light, Anna. *Be* the light."

There was a sudden gust of wind, and a familiar haunting cry sounded across the valley.

The Geese!

Startled, Anna Elizabeth and Mrs Johnson looked upwards and watched as the beautiful birds flew gracefully across the heavens. Their dark heads were clearly visible against the blue sky. Their mighty wings moved slowly up and down as they headed purposefully down towards the silent lake, which lay far below, still and at peace.

And then Anna Elizabeth knew what she had to do. She turned towards Mrs Johnson.

"I am so sorry for your loss," she said meaningfully.

Mrs Johnson's eyes filled with tears.

"Thank you," she replied.

Anna Elizabeth knew it was time for her to leave. She understood that Mrs Johnson should have the lookout rock for herself this morning, because she needed the healing the silent hill could give. Anna Elizabeth wanted her to have it.

She smiled and said, "Goodbye Mrs Johnson."

BEING THE LIGHT

Then she turned and ran down the hill. As she ran, Anna Elizabeth knew that there was something else she needed to do. Shell followed, and as they skidded and tripped on the small pebbles, Anna Elizabeth began to worry that she was not going to have enough time.

At the bottom of the hill, instead of turning to walk along the drive towards the house, she ran in the opposite direction towards the large gates of the estate. Shell ran beside her, his ears flapping, his pink tongue lolling. Anna Elizabeth's throat began to ache. She felt a sharp pain in her side, and she stopped to catch her breath, but only for a second. She wished she could run as fast as Isaac. She was fearful that she would be too late. On she ran. She saw the entrance to the estate in the distance. Just beyond lay the bus stop. As she ran, she could make out a solitary figure standing there. Joseph. She knew the bus was on its way and Joseph would be getting onto it. It would be taking him far away. Who knew when she would see him again?

When Anna Elizabeth began to think she would never make it in time, a car came rumbling up the drive from the house. She turned as it stopped beside her. The front window was open. Mother was driving.

"Get in," she said shortly to Anna Elizabeth.

Anna Elizabeth pulled open the back door. Everyone was squashed into the car. Gisela sat with Marta on her lap, Kornelia was beside her, and so was Isaac. Anna Elizabeth pushed Shell in, and he clambered onto Isaac. Then she squeezed in beside them and pulled the door closed. In the front seat, next to Mother, sat Lisi with the twins.

Mother cried, "Hold on everyone," and the car jerked forward.

It was not long before they had pulled up beside the lonely

figure standing at the bus stop. They all began to tumble out of the car. Joseph had been looking forlorn and lost, but now a look of relief washed over his face.

The bus that would be taking Joseph on the first leg of his journey into the unknown was already chugging along the road. Mother walked over to Joseph with her arms spread out towards him. Joseph welcomed her motherly embrace, and he returned it with warmth.

"I'm sorry," she said softly to him, her eyes glistening. "I know you must do what you believe you must do."

They hugged each other tight and then, moving reluctantly away from him, Mother called to Lisi.

"Come and say goodbye," she said.

Lisi held Joseph close, not wanting to let him go, but the twins were waiting. They were going to miss Joseph too. Finally, Lisi and Joseph let each other go, and he bent to hug the twins and all the other children. Anna Elizabeth saw tears flickering in Lisi's eyes, and she understood that she was trying to be brave. The bus rumbled closer, and as it drew up at the bus stop, Joseph pulled Anna Elizabeth towards him. He held her in a tight embrace without saying a word. Then letting her go, he bent down to stroke Shell.

"Look after Anna Elizabeth while I'm away, Shell," he said, his voice suddenly breaking. "Promise me you will!"

CHAPTER FOURTEEN

IN THE ICEHOUSE

The days and weeks seemed to fly by after Joseph's departure. Mother kept the children very busy with not only affairs around the village, but also with chores around the house. Anna Elizabeth saw her Mother in a new light. She had always dressed in soft and sweet-smelling, floating dresses. But now, as she took on tasks such as hoeing in the vegetable garden, chopping wood and feeding the pig, Anna Elizabeth noticed that she often dressed in blue, work overalls. Her soft, silk scarves, usually tied flimsily around her white neck, were now tied sturdily around her hair. It kept it from blowing in her face as she mucked out the stables, dug in the mud and mowed the meadow. At night, when she read to the children, she would struggle not to yawn, and as the weather grew colder, Anna Elizabeth saw that her smooth, white hands were dry and rough.

Normal lessons had started again at school, and brave Mrs Johnson managed to smile at each child every single day. Many times, during the months that followed, Anna Elizabeth saw the telegram boy cycling through the village. She always tried to take one of the white flowers growing up on the hillside to whichever family had received the sad telegram. The white flower never failed to make the recipient, smile faintly. Whenever Anna Elizabeth saw the smile, she remembered what her father had said.

"Be the light in the darkness, Anna. Be the light."

Anna Elizabeth hoped that she was doing as he had asked.

When the Stars Went On

With Father and Joseph both away that year, Christmas was a rather sad affair. Letters arrived sporadically from them both, and Anna Elizabeth sometimes saw Lisi pacing up and down the drive, in front of the house, waiting for the postman.

On Christmas day itself, there were not many gifts under the tree. The children had made the few delights that were there. Little Marta was given a small doll's house, which all the children had made for her using card and scraps of fabric and paint.

Kornelia, who was clever at handwork, had knitted each of the twins a pair of gloves for the winter. Lisi had altered an old shirt belonging to Father, to fit Isaac. He was growing so tall his wrists peeped out from the cuffs of his old shirt. There were no planes overhead and no warning whistles that Christmas day, and that felt like a gift to Anna Elizabeth.

Many weeks later, on one gloomy Saturday, it started to rain early in the morning. It rained and rained. And then it rained some more! Anna Elizabeth was frustrated. She hated being stuck in the house. Shell was longing to go for a walk, as he had missed his morning exercise. Isaac too, was keen to stretch his legs and run across the hills, breathing fresh air deep into his lungs.

After lunch, Mrs Eastwood walked into the front room. Anna Elizabeth was sitting on the red, cushioned window seat in the tall window, watching as the rain continued to stream down relentlessly. The puddles on the drive looked like bubbling, molten lead. Kornelia was knitting by the fire, Marta was playing with her new doll's house, and Gisela could be heard practising the piano in the next room. The twins were helping Mary in the kitchen, and Isaac was standing listlessly near Anna Elizabeth, staring at the grey sky.

"Oh, dear," said Mother. "I wish the rain would stop. I

promised Mrs Jenkins I would take her this fabric I have left from an old dress of mine. Maisy needs a new blouse. There is enough here to make one with room to grow."

"We'll take it, Mother," said Anna Elizabeth jumping up eagerly. "Oh, please let us go."

Isaac looked over at Mrs Eastwood, and his eyes lit up. Shell leapt to his feet, wagging his tail, and he whined softly. But Mother hesitated.

"It's very wet and cold out there," she said doubtfully.

"Oh, please Mother," begged Anna Elizabeth. "We can wrap up warmly."

At that very moment, a thin beam of sunlight broke through the cloud, so Mother relented.

"Well, alright. It looks as though the rain may let up for a while."

Anna Elizabeth and Isaac scrambled to get into their coats, and they clipped a lead onto Shell's collar. Taking the brown paper package from Mother, they skipped down the drive, splashing in the cold puddles as they went. They turned right and followed the path up the hill. It was slippery and muddy, but they laughed and squealed as they made their unsteady way upwards, higher and higher.

From the lookout rock, they could see that a soft, grey mist was hiding the lake from view, and the village was almost invisible. They half slipped, half tumbled down the other side of the hill, passing the icehouse before reaching the road leading to the Jenkins' house. They were both enjoying the freedom of the walk. Neither of them noticed that the door of the crouching icehouse was ajar!

By the time they reached the Jenkins' cottage, a rather thin sun was peeping through the clouds. Maisy invited them in. Anna Elizabeth handed Mrs Jenkins the package with the fabric inside. Together they opened it and spent a while admiring the pretty green, and blue stripe pattern, whilst Isaac played with Mittens, the cat.

"This is going to make such a pretty summer blouse for you," Mrs Jenkins said to Maisy as she bustled away to see to Max, who had a grisly cold.

Anna Elizabeth and Isaac got up to go.

"Stay a bit," begged Maisy. "It has been such a dreary day today. I could do with some company."

But Anna Elizabeth and Isaac had promised Mrs Eastwood that they would go straight home. They said polite goodbyes, and as the door closed behind them, they shivered. The sky was growing dark again.

"We must hurry," said Isaac.

They set off down the road through the village, towards the field leading up to the hill. They raced to beat the rain, but it was no good. Large drops began to splash down as they ran.

And then, the heavens opened. An icy sheet of blinding rain streamed down, obliterating their vision. There was a terrible flash of lightning followed by a deafening growl of thunder. Anna Elizabeth squealed. Together they fought to open the wooden gate at the bottom of the field.

"We must find cover," Anna Elizabeth wailed, as they ran across the field.

"The icehouse," yelled Isaac.

There was another mighty roar of thunder, and as it rolled and echoed around the hills, they stumbled blindly towards the icehouse. They made their way around to the door and for the first time, they saw that it was standing open. For a second, they hesitated. Anna Elizabeth was fearful.

"I don't want to go in," she cried.

But another clap of thunder forced them to scurry inside.

IN THE ICEHOUSE

Pulling Shell with them, they tumbled in, relieved to be out of the storm. It was dark and dry inside the icehouse, and it was silent after the terrible noise of the thunder. Anna Elizabeth and Isaac could not see anything. Their eyes needed to adjust to the darkness, but Shell began to growl. They looked at him in surprise. They had never heard Shell growl before.

The children noticed a smoky smell in the air. At the far end of the icehouse, a small, orange light began to glow. Someone was inside with them! Someone was smoking a cigarette in the icehouse. Anna Elizabeth gripped Isaac's arm, and Shell continued to growl. Then to their horror, a chesty cough reverberated through the icehouse, and they heard a voice.

"Visitors."

The children remained silent, too shocked to speak, but Shell's growl grew louder.

"Tell your dog to be quiet," said the voice sounding bored.

Anna Elizabeth crouched down beside Shell.

"Hush boy," she said to him.

He continued to growl softly. The howling wind blew the door open with a crash. At that exact moment, a forked bolt of lightning ruptured the darkness and illuminated the inside of the icehouse. The children could see that the gruff voice belonged to the missing pilot. There he sat, on the crate the children had used as a play table. He leaned against the red brick wall, wearing a blue pilot suit with large, brown, leather boots. He clasped a cigarette between two fingers. Isaac could feel his heart beating hard and fast in his chest, and Anna Elizabeth just managed to stifle a scream.

Terrified, they both turned to run back out into the storm, but the wind blew a mighty gust, and the door crashed shut. Together, in desperation, they tried to pull it open. They tugged and tugged at the door, but it remained jammed closed. They could hear the pilot moving in the darkness. He was closing the distance that separated them. They scrambled away and huddled down together in terror. Through the gloom, they could make out his face as he lurched and shuffled across the stone floor.

Gripping his cigarette between his teeth and with his left eye creased closed against the nicotine fumes, he walked over to the door. He tried to open it, but it remained shut fast. He pulled the door handle with both hands. Then he rattled it, gave the door a vicious kick, and he roared! It was stuck! They were all trapped inside together. He muttered furiously to himself. Turning to the children, he snarled venomously.

"Now you've done it!"

*

The two frightened children crouched on the stone floor. Shell lay between them, growling intermittently. They grew cold, and they both began to shiver violently. They could see the old overcoats lying on the floor on the other side of the icehouse. They wished they could put them on to keep warm, but they were too afraid to move. The pilot was pacing up and down.

"Surely Mother will come looking for us," whispered Anna Elizabeth.

Isaac nodded.

"I hope she think to come here," he replied.

"Quiet!" roared the pilot.

The children cowered back against the cold, red brick wall. He leaned down towards them.

"You had better hope I get out of here before you do," he snarled.

IN THE ICEHOUSE

His foul breath blew in their faces. Shell barked and snapped at him, and the pilot jerked away. He had had enough. He lunged forward and grabbed the dog by the collar, dragging him roughly to the other end of the icehouse. Shell yelped.

"Leave him!" cried Anna Elizabeth forgetting her fear and jumping up.

But the pilot tied Shell to a large iron ring in the wall. Ignoring Shell's distraught barks and yelps, he continued to pace up and down. Isaac pulled Anna Elizabeth, and she sat close to him, trying to get warm. She could not take her eyes off Shell.

The time seemed to drag by. Just when the children thought it could not get more cold or miserable, the sounds of the storm died down. They could no longer hear thunder, nor could they see any flashes of light under the door.

Suddenly they heard a booming voice outside. They looked at each other with wide eyes. Big Andy! The pilot took a nervous step closer to the children, and Shell began to bark wildly. Isaac jumped up and ran to the door. He began to bang on it, crying out for help. The pilot stood frozen to the spot, waiting to see what would happen next.

"I hear you," called the voice outside.

It was definitely Big Andy. He began to bang on the door in an attempt to break the handle, and open it. And then they heard another voice.

"That is Shell I hear barking," it said.

It was the Good Doctor. Isaac began to yell again, and Anna Elizabeth jumped up to join him. Together, Big Andy and the Good Doctor began to lunge heavily against the door from the outside. Over and over they crashed up against it.

Anna Elizabeth was never sure what happened next, but it seemed that as the door finally burst open, Isaac was knocked backwards onto the floor. The pilot leapt forward and grabbed her roughly. He had his arm around her neck. She screamed in terror as he pulled her and stood backed up against the far wall.

Big Andy and the Good Doctor both stumbled into the icehouse. They stopped, shocked when they saw Anna Elizabeth held fast by the pilot.

The Good Doctor spoke quietly but menacingly.

"Let her go," he said in German. "Let her go."

But the pilot did not answer. He did not seem to understand German at all. To everyone's horror, he pulled out a pistol and held it above his head for everyone to see.

"Get back," he snarled, "or the girl dies!"

Shell was still tied up, but was pulling hard to free himself. He twisted and yelped frantically. He shook his head wildly. Suddenly, he broke free and flew furiously across the room to leap up at the pilot. He wanted to rescue Anna Elizabeth. In the confusion that followed, a shot was fired into the darkness! The sound cracked deafeningly in the small space and was followed almost immediately by a frightful yelp, and a bloodcurdling cry.

Then everything went silent, and Anna Elizabeth found herself free to run to the Good Doctor, who was still standing, aghast, by the door.

Big Andy had tackled the pilot! He had seen what needed to be done, and with a thunderous cry of fury, had charged across the room. He had dived at the pilot with all his might, and powerfully pinned him to the ground. His face was white. He was shaking and breathing fast, but the pilot could not move. Anna Elizabeth looked around for Shell.

"Shell," she called urgently. "Shell, come here!"

She turned to Isaac.

"Where is Shell?" she asked panicking.

Isaac looked stricken. He was staring into the gloom of the icehouse. Anna Elizabeth followed his gaze. There, lying in a thin shaft of silver evening light, lay Shell. Anna Elizabeth screamed and ran to where her beloved dog lay.

But Shell did not move.

Chapter Fifteen

ISAAC IS THE LIGHT

Anna Elizabeth did not remember anything much after that. She awoke in bed many hours later and found herself in her own bedroom. She knew Mother was by her side and she could make out two shadowy figures, standing by the window. She could hear low voices murmuring.

"She is fine," she heard the voice of Good Doctor say. "She is fine, but she has had a terrible shock. She will need time to recover."

"Thank you, Doctor," said the other figure by the window.

Anna Elizabeth knew that voice. Father! Father was home! As her eyes began to focus, she saw him move towards her bed. He was dressed in uniform. Anna Elizabeth had never seen him in uniform before. He sat down on the chair beside her and seeing that she was awake, took her hand and smiled at her. His eyes were filled with worry.

"Hello," he said tenderly, and his pale blue eyes, so much like her own, crinkled into a kind but concerned smile. Anna Elizabeth began to cry.

"Shell," she sobbed clinging to Father. "Shell."

The next day the family gathered at the bottom of the back garden, outside the kitchen. Father himself had dug a deep hole on the other side of the lavender bushes. The twins slowly and solemnly carried Shell, wrapped in an old, clean sheet, past the roses and past the lavender bushes. They handed him over to Father. Anna Elizabeth thought her heart would break as she watched Father gently lower her beloved pet into the dark hole. The family stood quietly weeping, waiting for Father to shovel fresh, damp soil into the hole that held the silent Shell.

Isaac took a step towards Anna Elizabeth and looked into her distressed eyes. In his hands he held his small, threadbare jacket with the blue star embroidered onto the white armband. He had taken the icehouse key out of the inside pocket, and the jacket lay limp in his arms.

"May I give this to Shell?" he asked.

Anna Elizabeth nodded.

Isaac turned and walked to the little grave where he stood silently contemplating the white mound in the dark hole. He knelt. With infinite gentleness, Isaac laid his jacket with the blue star on the white armband, over the still, lifeless body of the dog.

"Thank you, Shell," he whispered.

*

In the weeks that followed, the pieces of the puzzle of the man in the icehouse began to make sense. Sitting in the kitchen with Lisi and Mary one day, Anna Elizabeth heard how the man had been neither a pilot nor a German after all! In spite of all the village rumours, the man in the icehouse was the nasty, mean thief who had been stealing from everyone. He had even stolen his blue overalls from the pilot who had crashed his plane. He was now locked up and would not be frightening anyone ever again.

To the surprise of everyone in the village, Big Andy emerged as the hero of the day.

"When that thief shot his pistol at Shell, Big Andy tackled him," said Mary.

When the Stars Went On

"He knocked the wind out of that dirty scoundrel, and made him let go of Anna Elizabeth! Thank goodness Big Andy is such a good, strong rugby player!"

Lisi nodded.

"It is a good thing that Big Andy noticed the door of the icehouse standing open. If he had not gone to get the Good Doctor to help him investigate, they would not have found the children!"

Mrs Turner shuddered.

"Who knows what could have happened," she said, shaking her head as she walked through the kitchen to the hall.

Anna Elizabeth did not want to listen anymore. She got up from the table and walked listlessly to the back door. She could see out across the garden, but she could not bring herself to walk down the garden path. She knew too well that just on the other side of the roses and lavender, lay the fresh grave. Isaac had planted white flowers from the hillside on the grave, and they now covered the dark soil with a gentle, misty cloud. Feeling her breathing quicken and the tears begin to hurt her eyes, she turned away.

Isaac passed her as she made her way upstairs.

"Let's go for a walk," he suggested.

Anna Elizabeth shook her head. She was not yet ready to climb the hill without Shell.

"Leave me alone," she said. "You don't understand."

*

One morning, many weeks later, Anna Elizabeth knew it was time for her to visit the lookout rock. She missed the geese, and she hoped to see them. She missed breathing in the clean, cool air at the top of the hill. She was worried that her heart would ache unmercifully without Shell beside her, but she wanted to stand and gaze across the lake. She needed to feel the peace that the stillness of the hill never failed to bring to her heart.

It was early in the morning as she made her way down the stairs and through the silent hall of Eastwood House. She found it almost impossible to leave without picking up Shell's lead, which still hung on the hallstand. But, she bravely opened the door, and set off to take a walk up the hill, alone.

At the lookout rock, Anna Elizabeth stood with her face turned upward. The air was cold, but there was no wind. For a long time she stood with her eyes closed, feeling a sense of comfort as the sun, rising slowly higher and higher, began to warm her. But no geese flew over that morning. Then Anna Elizabeth shifted her gaze and stared down at the lake in silence, alone with her thoughts, until a small movement behind her, startled her. She turned. It was Isaac, out on a morning run. He did not move closer. He did not want to intrude. She smiled wanly.

"Come on," she said beckoning to him. "Let's sit here for a while."

He moved forward and knelt to sit beside her. Together they sat in silence, staring at the beauty of the valley. Nothing stirred, not even the tops of the trees in the forest below. And then Isaac spoke.

"I want to tell you a story."

Anna Elizabeth looked at him. Then, as he seemed to be asking her permission to talk, she nodded her head. Isaac went on.

"I too, have had great sadness."

Isaac had never told anyone anything about his life before coming to live at Eastwood House. Anna Elizabeth listened.

When the Stars Went On

"It happened one night, before I came here," he went on. "I was home. I was sleeping. I woke when I heard a loud noise. I was very afraid. There was lots of shouting outside, and I could hear glass breaking. Then I heard my parents shouting downstairs. Never had I heard that before! Tata was telling Mama to stop. But she was worried. People were breaking shop windows and setting fire to everything. Mama wanted to go across the street to the shop belonging to Babcia and Dziadek, my grandparents. I heard her screaming at Tata to let her go."

Anna Elizabeth felt her throat tighten. She could hardly breathe. Isaac went on.

"I get out of bed," said Isaac, "and I go to window. I look down, and I see soldiers everywhere. I see my Mama. She did not see me. In the moonlight, I could see her eyes, so wild, so angry. Her hair was dark and blowing in the wind. She was screaming at the people. She was not afraid. Suddenly, there was loud shot."

Isaac faltered for a second. His next words were spoken brokenly.

"My Mama fell. Just like your beautiful Shell, my Mama fell."

Anna Elizabeth understood. She felt her heart begin to race. Her breathing quickened. Isaac had told her something that no one else knew. She looked deep into his eyes. Although she had thought she had no tears left with which to cry, there were suddenly many tears flowing down her cheeks. In the next few minutes of silence, Anna Elizabeth cried and cried and cried.

She cried for the loss of Shell. She cried for not having understood the suffering of Isaac. She cried with longing for Father and Joseph. And, although she did not know it, she cried for the loss of her childhood.

Then Isaac put his hand into his jacket pocket. He gently

held something out to her. She looked to see what it was. Lying in the palm of his hand was Tata's white handkerchief.

"It's clean," he said softly and shyly with a wry smile. "It always helps for tears."

"Oh Isaac," said Anna Elizabeth as she took the soft, linen handkerchief, "today in my darkness, you have been the light."

*

By September 1945, the 'stupid war' was over! There were great celebrations in the village. Mr Ellis, who had returned from the war with a dark patch over one eye, drove his old tractor through the village, pulling a cart filled with hay. Mrs Ellis, smiling joyfully, was seated beside him. All the young village children clambered up behind them, waving flags in celebration. But no child shone more in the eyes of the Eastwood household than little Marta, who waved her flag and laughed happily as the breeze pulled at the curling tendrils of her dark hair.

In December of that year, Hanukkah celebrations warmed the hearts of the children, and Christmas followed soon after. It was a joyous time. Eastwood House was glowing and bright. Father and Mr Jenkins brought in a huge tree from the estate, and once placed in the hall, the Jenkins children helped to decorate it.

On Christmas morning, Father, Mother, Joseph and Anna Elizabeth made their traditional frosty journey to the stone church in the village. By mid-morning, they were home again and gathered with everyone in the front room for elevenses. For Anna Elizabeth, it felt as though there was a small return to how things had been before the declaration of war, except that now, Lisi, standing close to Joseph, was wearing a small engagement ring on her left hand.

Kornelia had invited Big Andy and Mr Donley to visit. Since Big Andy had become the village hero, he and Kornelia had become great friends. Kornelia's fears had been forgotten, and they were deep in conversation. She had knitted him a scarf, which he was wearing even though the room was warm. Anna Elizabeth and Gisela were playing cards with the twins, and Mrs Eastwood was reading a story to Marta. There was a loud, cheerful knock at the front door.

"I wonder who that could be?" said Mother looking up.

Isaac went to answer the door, and presently the Good Doctor was ushered into the parlour.

"Merry Christmas," said Father, shaking his hand.

"Shalom," said the Good Doctor warmly.

"Won't you join us?" asked Father.

"Thank you," replied the Good Doctor, "but Mrs Bray has prepared a wonderful dinner, and I am going to be joining her. She has invited Mrs Johnson to join us. I can't be late."

"No, of course not," said Father smiling.

"But," continued the Good Doctor, "I had wondered if I could borrow Anna Elizabeth to carry in something for me."

Anna Elizabeth looked up with interest. Everyone was watching her.

"Oh yes," she said, jumping up. "Of course."

She followed the Good Doctor out of the room. She didn't notice that everyone silently stood up to follow her. In the hall, she found Isaac standing by the tall, glimmering Christmas tree, his face radiant. In his arms he was holding a tiny, sleepy, soft, golden spaniel.

"Oh!" said Anna Elizabeth as her eyes fell on the new arrival.

Isaac held the puppy out to her.

"For you," he said softly and shyly.

ISAAC IS THE LIGHT

Astonished, Anna Elizabeth looked around at everyone gathered in the hall. Their eyes were fixed upon her. Every one of them wanted her to be happy about the new puppy. Every one of them looked at her hopefully, willing her to adore the new arrival. Everyone understood that she had been lost without Shell, and they wanted her to reclaim something of the joy that she had buried with her beautiful, adored pet.

"How I love these people," she thought to herself, as she saw their smiling, hopeful faces.

Mother, Father, Joseph, Lisi, Gisela, Kornelia, Jacov, Zimeon, Marta and Isaac, as well as Big Andy and the Good Doctor.

"My family," she sighed happily to herself, "gifted to me by the stupid war."

Anna Elizabeth walked over to Isaac and reached out to take the tiny, warm bundle into her arms. She held the small, snuffling creature to her face and she kissed his soft, golden fur. Her family breathed a collective sigh of happiness and grinned broadly.

"Oh," she said again, her eyes shining. "I shall call you, Star!"

More books by this author

- Tragear's Grotto
- Major Oak
- Pig, Pug 'n' Persian

If you enjoyed this book, please take a few moments to leave a review on Amazon.

Thank you so much,
Anne.

For more information, visit www.annedewaal.co.uk

ABOUT THE AUTHOR

Anne de Waal was born in East London, South Africa in 1963. The first six years of her life were spent in this sunny, windy seaside town. In 1969 her family moved up north to the gold mining world of Johannesburg. She was educated at Horison View Primary School and Westridge High School. Aged seventeen, she decided to study music seriously, and she completed her schooling at Johannesburg Art, Ballet, Drama and Music School. She went on to receive her degree at the University of the Witwatersrand.

In 1987 she married musician Dana de Waal, and together they toured the country making music. Their daughter was born in 1989 and their son, in 1990. In 2001 the family emigrated to the United Kingdom where they settled in Derbyshire.

She and her husband continue to make music and teach all over the United Kingdom. Together, they run Derby Music Academy.

When the Stars Went On is her first novel for children.

Printed in Great Britain
by Amazon